Frederik Sandwich and the
Earthquake that Couldn't Possibly Be

FREDERiK SANDW!CH

and the

EARTHQUAKE

that Couldn't

PoSSIBLY

BE

Kev!n John Scott

sourcebooks
jabberwocky

Published by Sourcebooks Jabberwocky,
an imprint of Sourcebooks, Inc.
P.O. Box 4410, Naperville, Illinois 60567-4410
(630) 961-3900
Fax: (630) 961-2168
sourcebooks.com

The Library of Congress has cataloged the hardcover edition as follows:

Names: Scott, Kevin John, author.
Title: Frederik Sandwich and the earthquake that couldn't
possibly be / Kevin John Scott.
Description: Naperville, Illinois : Sourcebooks Jabberwocky, [2018] |
Summary: A completely implausible earthquake sets Frederik Sandwich and
Pernille, a mysterious stranger, on an adventure through secret and forbidden
places in their small town.
Identifiers: LCCN 2017008281 | (alk. paper)
Subjects: | CYAC: Adventure and adventurers--Fiction. | Underground
areas--Fiction. | Earthquakes--Fiction. | Toleration--Fiction. | Mystery
and detective stories.
Classification: LCC PZ7.1.S336847 Fre 2018 | DDC [Fic]--dc23 LC record
available at https://lccn.loc.gov/2017008281

Source of Production: Berryville Graphics, Inc., Berryville, Virginia, United States
Date of Production: November 2018
Run Number: 5013627

Printed and bound in the United States of America.
BVG 10 9 8 7 6 5 4 3 2 1

For Milo and Sam

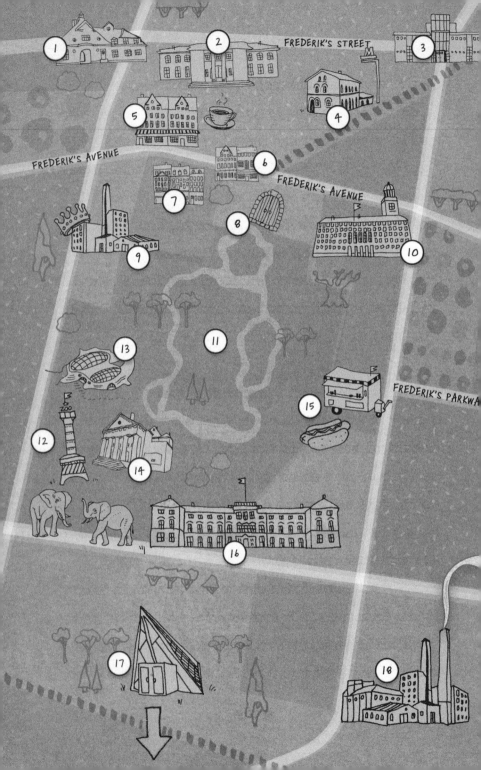

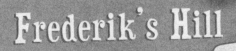

Frederik's Hill

Prologue

*Eleven Years before the Earthquake
that Couldn't Possibly Be*

O n Frederik's Hill by King Frederik's Garden Park there lived a boy named Frederik. His parents had simply run out of ideas, exhausted and overjoyed as they were in the aftermath of his birth, in Frederik's Hospital, overlooking Frederik's Shopping Mall, at the end of Frederik's Street.

"A boy," the midwife announced, and what other name was to hand?

On Frederik's Hill that royal name was given to almost everything, and Mr. and Mrs. Sandwich didn't wish to stand out, thank you, new to the country, neighbors eyeing them with suspicion. They wanted to blend in, shop in Frederik's

Fruit and Veg, sip coffee at Frederik's Café while gazing across Frederik's Square at the statue of King Frederik the Fifth—or was it the Fifteenth? No one quite recalled, there having been so many King Frederiks over the centuries in an orderly succession: Frederik, William, Frederik, William, like the ticktock of a clock. In the sprawling city beyond the Hill, the Williams were much preferred. Hence William's Castle, William's Wharf, and William's Seaside Strand. But Frederik's Hill rose above the city beyond and thought itself a trifle better, a separate borough with separate traditions despite having long been engulfed by the city beyond on every side. On Frederik's Hill, for as long as anyone had set down records, the line of Frederiks was celebrated.

Mrs. Sandwich gazed at the baby's folded-up face and tried to read some sign of who he might become, this miniscule mite, minutes old. She tried to think of something original. But history was against her, as she knew. Alfonso's Apothecary had lasted a winter, but nobody had bought his remedies. Not with trusty Frederik's Medicines just along Frederik's Street. Locals had cured their sniffles with Frederik's Medicines all their lives, despite the despot behind the counter, whose name wasn't Frederik at all, by the way.

❦ × ❧

Balthazar's Boulangerie went the same way, in business for a week or two, till the bread went bad and barely a toe had crossed the threshold. There were buns and loaves to be had around the corner at Frederik's Breadsticks. Balthazar's window offered riches in pastry and glaze, beautiful Berliners, scrumptious scones, cherries and nuts on top of everything. Frederik's Breadsticks offered little that wasn't dry and sorry and stale. But the *name* was dependable; the *name* could be trusted. The wares were immaterial.

The exhausted mother, hair matted against her forehead, held her wrinkled bag of a boy and peered through a misted window, and all she could see in any direction were Frederiks, Frederiks, and more Frederiks.

"Have you thought of a name for your little boy?" the midwife asked from the foot of the bed.

"I can think of only one," she replied.

CHAPTER 1

Alone Alone

Fiddle-lick! Fiddle-lick Sore-itch!"

"My name is *Frederik*," Frederik snapped. "Frederik *Sandwich*." He was seething. Wanted to pop. It made him boiling mad and they knew it. A posse of predatory kids at the pedestrian crossing. Their lips twitched. Eyes moistened. Spit was sprayed. Sides were grasped—they were laughing, howling, uncontrollably. At him. Every one of them. Frederik Grevsen, Frederik Faurholt, Frederik Dahl Dalby, and not just the Frederiks either. Erik the Awkward. Erica Engel. Calamity Claus, his arm in a sling again. All of them. Hooting. It was always like

this. He wanted to fold in on himself and disappear, be far away, have someone—anyone—be *kind*.

"What's so funny?"

He never knew. Had never ever understood. Frederik was the single most common name on Frederik's Hill.

"*Fiddle-lick!*" wailed Erica Engel.

"Flipper-rack!" Frederik Grevsen chortled.

They dabbed at their cheeks. Exchanged high fives. With everyone but him.

A sharp wind whipped along the long street. It made noses run like crazy. But was anyone mocking that? No! Just his name. Only his. And half of them had the same one!

This had been happening for years. To Frederik alone.

He was always alone.

And yet no one else was. The neighboring kids hung around in a great big pack of great big pals. Only Frederik was left out. And why? Was he any different than them? No! He had spent his early childhood doing the same as them: exploring, experimenting, nothing much on his mind beyond forward and backward and *ooh, I wonder what's under here*. He had learned to walk like them and talk like them. In two different languages actually. And that was the one thing that seemed to set him apart. The one thing was the two languages. There was one for everyday outdoor usage and another his parents used at home. Nobody else understood that one, so he kept it quiet. He tried to mask any trace of his family's peculiar accent. He spoke almost exactly like a local. He *was* a local. He had *the* most popular local name. So what, in fact, was so funny? What was their *point*?

"Froller-rock!"

"Flabby-wreck!"

"Stop it! That is *not* how I said it!"

The traffic lights changed. Dabbing their eyes, chuckling still, the neighbors peeled away, across the street, heading home, leaving Frederik by himself. Just like every day.

He had to follow after them. Home was that way. Buses and bicycles rumbled and rattled, ready to race away the moment the lights were green. The street was a canyon of orderly buildings stretching to the sunset. Old, plastered tenement blocks, six floors high. A thousand wood-framed windows reflecting a fire-red sky. He passed the duck pond, the blue house, and the yellow. Holding back. Humiliated. He caught the whispers of their laughter on the breeze.

Past Frederik's Fruit and Veg. A glance through the window of Frederik's Antiques.

And then all the children ahead of him stopped. Abruptly.

He hesitated. Stopped too. Didn't want to get too close.

Across the street, outside the Café Grondal, well-dressed women huddled under blankets, sipping cocoa at ornate tables. Gretchen Grondal, proprietor, pillar of the community, busybody, paused from taking orders and peered at the children as if to say standing in the street is against the rules.

But the children didn't care about the rules—not at that moment. For standing tall, very tall actually, outside the shop on the corner of his street, was the weird girl.

Frederik didn't know her name. No one did, as far as he was aware, and given her appearance, it was probably unpronounceable. She lived right there, above the upholsterer's workshop, a jumble of fabrics and furniture behind vast plate glass that reflected every passerby like a mirror, splashing sunlight in all directions when the weather was right. She had evidently just got home from school, though Frederik didn't know which school she went to.

She didn't speak. She eyed the watching children

with open disdain. She examined a fingernail, twisted a few strands of her weird white hair in a knot, tossed her head, and turned away to her door.

The weird girl was weird.

Everyone said so.

She acted weird. Looked weird. Dressed weird. Therefore *was* weird. Hard to argue. Weird white hair. Weird skin too. Dark. Not just a tan from a skiing vacation or an evening or two in a tanning bed. Not that kind of dark. Something much more permanent. Something foreign. On Frederik's Hill, foreign was definitely, definitively weird. The white hair could be local enough, but the dark skin, no. And the two did not go together.

The girl stepped quickly inside the upholsterer's workshop. The door slammed behind her. The window rattled. Frederik watched her recede behind the shine of the glass. She merged with the shadows and was gone. Like a ghost.

"Weirdo," said Erica Engel.

"They should all be kicked out, my dad says," Erik the Awkward added. "All the foreigners." And the whole group pivoted. Suddenly. To stare.

At Frederik.

He took a few steps back. A chill in his belly all over again. "Yes," he said. He tried to laugh. It didn't come out in the least bit convincingly. "Maybe they should," he said and was instantly ashamed of himself for agreeing with bullies.

"Who wants them?" Frederik Dahl Dalby murmured.

"What good are they?" Frederik Faurholt.

"Not welcome," Frederik Grevsen, under his breath.

"What do *you* think, Fiddle-rack?" Erica Engel sneered.

"I don't know," he said. "I expect you're right. She's weird, that weird girl. Don't you think? I think so. Definitely. Weird."

He was sweating. It wasn't hot. He was shivering too, and it wasn't cold, not for frosty Frederik's Hill on a breezy spring afternoon. They would notice him sweating and shivering, and then it would get worse. He tried another chuckle but no one chuckled with him. All those faces, fair and freckled, a line of blue eyes, unblinking. Cold, blue eyes fixed on Frederik.

"*I'm* from here," he added, desperate now. "From Frederik's Hill."

A single snort of scorn from Erica Engel. Knowing looks among the boys.

"Should all be kicked out, my dad says," Erik the

Awkward muttered again, and they all moved a pace or two closer. Frederik stepped off the edge of the sidewalk to get around them, to get away. There were shouts from behind. A blizzard of bicycles whipping by, bells ringing furiously, harsh words, shaken fists. On Frederik's Hill, there were hundreds of cyclists, thousands of them, everywhere. You never *ever* stepped off the sidewalk without looking. He had almost caused a horrific accident. He dropped his face in shame and ran for the corner, past the upholsterer's, toward his house, a block away, where he could be *alone* alone.

"Catch you tomorrow, Flabby-wick," someone called at his back.

He didn't turn to find out who. Whoever it was, they were no friend of his. Frederik didn't have a friend in the world. He had never understood why, though he knew it was somehow because of his name and the way he said it. And a little part of him, deep inside, longed to object, to shake things up, to really rock the boat—to stop them mimicking him and mocking him and making him miserable. But it wasn't done. It wasn't allowed. No matter how much a shake-up might be needed, a shake-up was the very last thing that could happen on sensible, rule-following Frederik's Hill.

CHAPTER 2

The Earthquake that Couldn't Possibly Be

At the age of eleven or thereabouts, Frederik suddenly woke up. Of course, he had awoken before at a whole range of ages, three for example, eight and a half, and everything in between on an orderly, daily basis. There was nothing unusual about awakening at the age of eleven apart from the violent shaking. The bed was shaking. Violently. Like an airplane in turbulence. The whole room. Rippling and shuddering. Frederik, at first, was unruffled. He had been asleep in a world of dreams where unusual things happen all the time, and this was another unusual thing and therefore entirely to be expected. Except he was

awake. When Frederik worked that out, he became rapidly ruffled after all.

The room was dark. Through slats in the blinds, streetlights made stripes on the ceiling. The stripes were vibrating.

"Aaaagh," said Frederik, to see if he could, to make sure this wasn't one of those dreams where he thought he was awake but really wasn't. But sure enough, the sound came out in a warble.

"Aaaagh," he said again, and this time it wasn't an experiment but a creeping doubt. Pictures clattered and the bed shook like a washing machine. How long had this been going on? A minute? More? He could still remember his dream and there had been no shaking—not till he awoke abruptly to find his bed on the move.

He tried to make sense of this unprecedented situation, not daring to budge. His room took up the top floor of a tall, narrow house. His parents slept four floors below in their basement bedroom—they found it cozy. Frederik meanwhile felt a glorious freedom up here in the rafters. He loved to lean from the balcony and stare over rooftops, between chimneys, tracking time by the clock tower that looked like a lighthouse but couldn't possibly be because the sea was too far away. He could gaze at the stars through his telescope and feel like he was among them, part of a never-ending, orderly pattern. Up here, there were no unpleasant neighbors, no one he had to avoid. But tonight, all alone halfway to the sky with everything rattling, he felt for the first time entirely too far from the ground.

In the shadows, he could see only shapes—the end of the bed, the wardrobe. The silhouette of his precious telescope as it fell off its stand and rolled to the edge of the dresser. He reached out a hand in dread but was too far away. The telescope tipped, a dead weight of metal and delicate glass. It hit the hardwood floor with a thud and a tinkle of broken pieces. His most treasured possession!

Frantic, frightened, and fascinated, all on top of one another, he scrambled to get up and check outside. Hesitated—afraid of what might be out there. Tanks invading the streets and shaking the city off its foundations. No. Nothing like that had happened in generations. And tanks would be noisy. Beyond the rattling blinds and his property smashing, there was no sound. No far-off rumble, no nearby clatter. No thunder, no gunfire, and still the furniture jolted as though the building had been loaded on a truck and driven down an unpaved road.

There had to be a sensible explanation, and his next thought was an earthquake. But Frederik's Hill was built on silt and sand and thousands of miles from anything so dramatic, a pimple on the lowest, dullest island of a stable, orderly nation. No faults, no rifts, no volcanoes—nothing but shallow sea and sandy soil. No earthquake had been recorded here in the history of science, and Frederik knew his science, studied it diligently. An earthquake it couldn't possibly be.

And then a terrible, new suspicion crept in under his guard.

Aliens.

Massive, silent spaceships in the sky above his bedroom, pounding the planet with wobble rays to break the spirits of the inhabitants of Earth. Tremble beams, shaking the town like a tambourine. Sinister creatures with tentacle fingers and almond-shaped eyes. The city surrounded in three dimensions, maybe more. All would perish. Skinned, pureed, and poured into a stinking vat on the mother ship to be slowly digested in the awful acid of alien stomachs. He knew this to be fanciful and foolish, but what other interpretation was there? It scared the bejeebers out of him.

He wrestled loose from the warmth of his quilt. He crawled like a commando across the bed, head low, riding the shudders that clattered his windows and toppled his belongings. He reached for the blinds, tilted the slats, and peered out through condensation and glass and cold night air.

And the trembling stopped.

There was nothing. No shudders, no aftershocks. No rattling, no falling possessions. In the distance a dog barked. Just once.

He scanned the night sky. No spaceships. No swirling lights. Just cloudy night. The rooftops, the factory chimney climbing out of the darkness, and the clock tower on top of Municipal Hall that looked like a lighthouse but couldn't be. The shaking stopped so suddenly, it seemed to Frederik he had stopped it himself when he opened the blind. He twisted the slats to see if he could start it again. But there was nothing, and besides, it made no sense. Nothing made sense. It wasn't a dream and it wasn't spaceships and it couldn't possibly be an earthquake. And still the building had nearly shaken itself apart.

And then Frederik detected a new noise, a groaning of floorboards, a creak on the stairs. Something was coming. Out on the landing, coming closer, coming for Frederik with tentacle fingers, to squeeze out his insides and spin them into thread and use them to floss giant, jagged teeth. He hid behind the bed, in dust and pieces of broken telescope, covering his head with his hands. His heartbeat hammered in his ears. The door groaned open.

"Aaaagh," he said for the third time, and it proved the most convincing of the three. He held his breath and screwed his eyes shut and prepared to be liquefied.

There was a horrible pause.

"Frederik?" said his mother, panicky. "You're on the floor! Are you all right? Were you hurt in that awful earthquake?"

Frederik, hugely relieved, took a long moment to compose himself.

"It wasn't an earthquake," he said, clinging grimly to all he knew. "It couldn't possibly be."

But even so, after eleven years of perfectly predictable nighttimes, Frederik had been shaken shockingly awake.

CHAPTER 3

A Faceful
of Muggy Wind

And then the weird girl started following him. Not in the middle of the night, of course, but next morning, on his way to the train. She was irrationally tall and talkative. She followed him across the square.

"An earthquake," she said. "Imagine!"

"It was not an earthquake," he explained. "It couldn't possibly be." He tried to sound sure of himself, but it came out slightly pompous. "All will be explained, I'm certain. Watch the news or something."

"The news?" the weird girl replied. "Goodness no. They tell you whatever they want you to believe."

An icy wind rushing in from the unseen sea nipped at his cheeks and ears. He should have worn a woolly hat, a point his mother had pointed out as he paid no attention on his way to the door.

"They tell you the *news*," he said. "You're not from around here. What could you possibly know?"

He didn't mean to be mean, but she wasn't making sense, she was weird, and he was in a rush.

"I most certainly am from around here," the girl said. "And I could know a great deal. I could be a volcanologist."

"Or a half-wit," Frederik muttered. It came out harshly. But in his defense, he was late for the train, and that would make him late for school. He hated to be late for school, and especially today. Today was going to be far too important to miss. They would surely find out what had caused all that shaking. Whatever could it have been?

The stairs leading down from the square to the platform were clogged with people.

"By my calculations, a 4.7 on the Richter scale," said the girl, determinedly at his heels. "I found a handy do-it-yourself template on the internet."

"Stop following me," said Frederik.

She grabbed his collar and trotted behind him, down the steep steps, chattering, pulling the neck of his coat till he thought he might choke.

"Using," she said, "the handy do-it-yourself template I found on the internet, I place the epicenter of the earthquake at a shallow depth directly below Frederik's Hill."

Frederik had heard entirely enough. At the foot of the stairs, he slipped her grip and hurried into the crowd. *Richter scale*, for goodness sake. Frederik owned an encyclopedia, a computer, and until very recently, a rather good telescope. The first thing he had checked in the night, after picking himself up out of the dust and promising to go back to sleep, was the seismic history of the Hill. There wasn't one. No mention of anything. Earthquakes, as he'd suspected, owing to the utter absence of faults, fissures, or magma pockets, could never occur within a thousand miles.

He picked his way along the platform. It was narrow and dark. Pillars supported a blackened ceiling. People everywhere, jammed together, as far as he could see in the underground gloom. A woman was leaning against a *No Smoking* sign. She teased a cigarillo from a pocket and held it to her lips. Heads snapped in her direction, murmurs of outrage. On Frederik's Hill, the rules were strictly adhered to. She hurried it out of sight and sidled away, shamefaced.

From somewhere far beyond, there came a burst of gruff shouting. "Padma! Padma?" Nobody paid the slightest attention. That sort of thing wasn't encouraged either.

Frederik drifted out toward the edge and the dangerous drop to the railway line. Litter floated in oily pools between the rails. The wall beyond was one vast billboard. It read *Her Ladyship the Mayor's International Midsummer Festival*. There were pictures of smiling children. Fireworks and spectacular fountains. Her Ladyship the Mayor was the guiding light of Frederik's Hill. She had been in office longer than Frederik had been alive. If there was one person who wouldn't stand for any nonsense about earthquakes, it was Her Ladyship, and thank goodness for that.

A group of boys flirted with the edge of the platform. He realized too late who they were.

"An *earthquake*," said Erik the Awkward. "My house barely survived!"

"I was almost killed," said Calamity Claus. "By falling shoes."

"This one was only a tremor," Lars Jacobsen said. "A warning. The next one could wipe out civilization entirely!"

Frederik knew to keep his distance from these boys, an understanding they had reached very early in his schooling. They didn't speak to him except to insult him and expected him not to speak to them in return. Frederik had been raised to do what people expected, and so that was pretty much that. But was today perhaps an exception? They were frightened and worried. He could tell. Who wouldn't be? And Frederik knew a thing or two about this stuff. This was a chance to give back to his community, wasn't it? A chance to be a part of something bigger. A chance to belong.

"Seismically speaking," he said, stepping forward, "the tectonic undertexture of our bedrock provides no instabilities, so we have to deduce that it *wasn't* in fact an earthquake." He smiled a reassuring smile. "It couldn't possibly be."

The boys gazed back at Frederik as one might examine dog deposits on the underside of a shoe.

"Did someone talk to him?" asked Lars.

"Not me," said Claus.

"Private conversation," said Erik the Awkward. "Skedaddle, Sandwich. You're not one of us."

"I *am* one of us," he pointed out, wounded.

But the boys weren't listening at all. Instead, they were staring past him. At the weird girl.

She was standing at Frederik's shoulder with her inconsistent hair and skin combination. "Sandwich?" she said. "How delightful. You're named after a foodstuff. Tell me, do they always ostracize you so bluntly?"

"No," Frederik snapped at her. "Go away."

"I certainly shall not go away," she said. "I'm here to help you in your hour of need."

"I don't want your help."

But the boys were already peeling away, laughing cruelly. And just like that, just like always, Frederik found himself shunned. Rejected. He backed away, trying to look like he wasn't bothered: a look he had practiced for many years but which still didn't fool anyone. He folded into the crowd feeling small and wretched and furious with that girl for interfering. Just when he might have made an impression!

There was a rush of thick air, an electric hum, and a train eased in on the westbound line, the wrong direction for Frederik. The train was sleek and modern and shiny. The doors slid aside with a sigh. People battled their way on and off. There was some unhelpful pushing. Pushing was against the rules as well. Had everyone gone mad today? Had that shaking gone to their heads?

He picked past businessmen and baby carriages. He stood as close as he dared to the edge. He didn't speak to anyone. He would do what he always did. He'd get on the train and away from them all, find a seat by himself.

A man picked up a briefcase and peered into the tunnel. A woman gripped her child's little hand and stood on tiptoe to see the arrivals board. It counted down in increments— one minute till the next train, thirty seconds. People tensed, packed tight. Frederik stuck his face farther out, over the edge, staring to his right and into darkness. Three lights in a triangle, getting brighter, coming closer. A faceful of muggy wind and the hum of the rails and a sudden, sickening lurch. The crowd surged and the floor shook, and Frederik was slipping and it wasn't an earthquake, couldn't possibly be, but he was tumbling and losing his feet and his head stuck out from the crush and twenty seconds away, fifteen, ten, the flat face of the onrushing train. He was toppling into open air, over the edge, in the path of the seven twenty-two, all stations to William's Harbor. Bright light bore down, litter lifted and twisted in the dirt, and the hum of the train became a terrible roar. He flailed for a handhold and just as the train came close enough to see the whites of the driver's eyes, there was a hefty tug and Frederik was pulled from the path of the train and back to the platform.

He fell to one knee, cracked it hard against the tiles. His eyes watered, he scuffed his shoe, and before he could worry what his mother would say, before he even caught his breath, there were bony fingers in his hair and a burst of pain. Frederik yelped, down on his knees on the platform. A cold cheek pressed against his. Weird white hair at the edge of his vision and a high-pitched voice, too close, too loud in his ear, saying, "Now who's the half-wit, muffin dear?"

CHAPTER 4

Railroaded

The weird girl had big eyes—too big—and he wanted them out of his face. Big, blinking eyes with big, black pupils and blue around the black and flashes of orange darting through the edges. She had little laser-sharp dark-brown freckles. Frederik hated freckles. Frederik had freckles of his own, and his mother called them "angel kisses," and his father called them "snot spots," and he wasn't sure which was worse. He hated freckles, he was thoroughly embarrassed, and he was going to miss his train.

He jumped up as best he could among the legs and bags. He tore his backpack out of the tangle and made for

the open door of the carriage, a short distance and a great many bodies away.

"Wait for me," said the weird girl.

"No," said Frederik.

She took a tight hold of his sleeve, and his momentum was abruptly checked.

"You know," she shouted above the clamor, "the wisest sages of China say that when a life is saved there is a lifelong debt. And yet, it is not the one rescued who owes that debt. It is the rescuer herself!"

A man in a black mood and a red raincoat blocked Frederik's path. An old woman elbowed him. He was hemmed in by people on cell phones, people with headphones, none of them paying the least regard.

"A lifelong debt," the girl announced in his ear. "I saved your life and I will strive forever to repay you."

"Get away from me," said Frederik.

A shrill whistle, a final crush, and amid the commotion an eruption of curses, a guttural, asthmatic cough. Everyone paused for a moment, looked from side to side, and then renewed their scramble for the carriage. Frederik made a lunge, but his sleeve was still in the girl's grasp and the people in front wouldn't budge, and as he reached out to elbow his way through, there was a clunk and a hiss and the doors slid closed in a rush. Faces inside pressed against glass and stared at the faces left on the platform. The electric whine climbed an octave and the train began to roll, slipping sideways past Frederik's outstretched hand into the blackness of the tunnel.

"Bother," said the girl. "Now you've made me miss my train."

"What?" said Frederik, outraged. "You made *me* miss *mine*!"

"Well, I hardly think so," said the girl. "If not for me, you'd have fallen in front of it. You'd be broken bones and raspberry jam smeared all over the tracks. Your head would be crushed like a rotten pumpkin and your torso sliced into two or three parts. Your eyeballs would have popped out on impact and landed in somebody's hair, and do you know the price of a decent shampoo and blow-dry in this day and age? I didn't make you miss the train. I made the train miss you! If not for me, you'd be underneath it, splattered all over the driver's windshield, dangling in bits from the undercarriage."

"Please!" said Frederik, queasy. "That's enough. I'm grateful. I owe you."

"On the contrary," said the girl. "I owe *you*."

He tried to edge away again. He couldn't be seen with the weird girl. People spurned him enough already! But it somehow didn't seem right to ignore her completely. She had pulled him from the path of a locomotive.

"If it wasn't an earthquake," she announced, "we must find out what it was. Don't you agree?"

"No," he told her, though actually she was right.

He checked all around to make sure those boys hadn't seen him talking to her. They were gone. On the train he had missed. What time was it? Was he late? He'd never missed his train before. He had no idea when the next one was due.

The weird girl stepped toward the giant billboard beyond the tracks. "Her Ladyship's international festival," she said. "Just weeks away. If the shaking should happen again, the event will be ruined. Think of those VIP guests, shaken like rattles, crushed by rubble—their gowns besmirched, their hats awry, their VIP blood seeping slowly into the soil. We must prevent it at all costs!"

"You really are weird," said Frederik.

"I really am serious. We must find the cause of the shaking at once, for the sake of the mayor."

"*Imbeciles!*" An explosion of shouting and a hacking cough immediately behind them. "*Idiots!*"

Frederik stared, startled, at the weird girl. She stared back, her eyes bigger than ever. "Who said that?" she said.

As if in answer, a head was lowered sideways into the space between them. A red, rude face, all beastly beard and bad breath and boils and warts and nose hairs. The foul old man gave a fearsome belch and the air grew thick with onions.

"For the sake of the *mayor*?" snarled the man. "That *monster*?"

His coat was worn and matted with what looked and smelled like animal dung. He was clearly some kind of bum or tramp. There were holes in his gloves and stains on his pants, and his shoes were quite unspeakable.

Frederik quietly took a very tight grip on his backpack. "I'm sorry," he said, as he had been taught to do in such circumstances. "Not today. Thank you." He averted his eyes and stepped aside and waited for the old man to shuffle off and worry someone else.

"*Sorry?*" the man growled, leaning close with his terrible breath. It was all Frederik could do not to gag. "You'll be sorry when her zombies rise from the bowels of the hill!"

"Zombies?" said Frederik, alarmed.

"Hideous gargoyles! Lurking in the darkness. Legions of them. They will gut you like dogs and sell your kidneys for castanets! You felt that earthquake. They have awoken! Get aboveground! Board up the exits!" He looked alarmingly directly at Frederik from close proximity.

"It wasn't an earthquake."

"Of *course* it wasn't! It was them! Stirring after all these years. It will be like it was before! Exactly the same all over again. They never went away! When will it change? When will there ever be *change*?"

"Please go away," Frederik managed. "I don't have any change. And besides, begging is against the rules."

"Whose rules?" the old man erupted. "Her rules! The mayor's rules!"

"Go away," Frederik said, trying to hide his extreme unease. "Go away or I shall call for a policeman."

The old man took in an enormous volume of air. It

rattled and bubbled in his chest. His face became redder than ever.

The weird girl was staring, frightened for sure but also enraged. Eyes narrowed, lips tight. Frederik didn't want to be here. But he didn't want to embarrass himself again by running away. So he set his jaw very firmly in the way tough guys do when faced with such moments in movies. It was all he could think of.

"My father knows the chief of police for Frederik's Hill," he said, and this was true because his father had met the chief of police on civic business and also once in Frederik's Fresh Produce. His father had allowed the chief the last carton of yogurt. If that wasn't a debt, Frederik didn't know what was. That was a real debt, and it was clear who owed it to whom.

"That dribbling nostril?" the old tramp scoffed. "The chief of police for Frederik's Hill? The mayor's lackey lapdog? The chief of police for Frederik's Hill is a toadying timeserver and typical of this two-faced tin-pot tightwad town!"

"I mean it," Frederik told the old man, though he was far from sure he did. "I'll set the authorities on you."

"Then I," said the man, "will leave you down here, at

the mercy of such horrors as you have never dared imagine. Do you think the *authorities* are the scary thing around here? Run while you can, before the mayor's miserable minions rise from the sewers and disembowel you and do us all a favor." And he added a small, smelly burp for emphasis.

The weird girl prodded the tramp's enormous shoulder, risking tetanus, Ebola, E. coli. "I will not have it!" she snapped at him. "I draw the line! I, ooh, I, ooh." She wagged her finger furiously. "Her Ladyship the Mayor is a role model to young women, I'll have you know!"

The tramp hissed in derision.

"She is!"

There was a *ding-dong* from the rafters and a garbled announcement. Frederik turned to the mouth of the tunnel, willing a train to arrive—any train. It didn't matter, the right direction or the wrong direction. At this point, he'd board it just to get away, even if it made him late, even though his first class was science and would be even more interesting than usual with an earthquake that couldn't possibly be to diagnose. He could feel the first licks of a breeze against his face, saw glimmers of light in the tunnel. The noise of the train rose from a rumble to a howl.

But the train he saw coming was not the train he expected.

They were usually slim and sleek and new, dark windows in clean, white carriages, quiet electric doors.

The train rolling into the eastbound platform was not sleek or new or clean or electric, but old and filthy and blue, belching thick diesel fumes that billowed under the arched ceiling and tumbled into the crowd. There were coughs and splutters, faces turned away, hands held over mouths. Frederik buried his face in his collar, but the fumes were nothing, a mere annoyance, compared with the incredible noise. The locomotive was long and stout, and it thundered like a hundred jackhammers. He had seen this train before on occasions. He couldn't imagine why it was allowed through Frederik's Hill. Clearly it came from some other borough, somewhere a lot less particular. He clamped his hands over his ears, and it was a good thing he did because the train began to screech—a howling squeal of brakes, needles of noise that slipped through his fingers and stabbed his eardrums. Bystanders backed away, mouthing complaints that could not be heard, and Frederik wanted to back away too but he couldn't! That foul old tramp was right behind him. What did he *want*? The blue train lurched to a halt, hissing.

A deafening clatter swept the length of the old blue train and every door burst open.

Nobody got off. Nobody got on. There seemed to be no one on board.

Frederik's Hill, said the sign. *Train Terminates Here.*

But a train that stopped here couldn't stop here for long. It had to get out of the way of the next and the next after that. On Frederik's Hill, timetables were strictly adhered to. He could feel the tramp's hot breath on the back of his neck. What if he just got on, rode to the next stop, and waited for the right train there? Escaping the tramp. Escaping the weird girl too! He took a deep breath, grabbed the handrail, and pulled himself smartly up three steep steps, into the grubby carriage, and immediately, instantly, realized this was completely against the rules. He, Frederik, was *breaking the rules* in front of at least a hundred people.

He turned back in panic but the filthy old tramp was reaching after him, yelling, ranting, "Don't ride that train! Get *off*! You don't know what's down there!"

And the weird girl was waving and shouting, "Wait for me, wait for me!" She sidestepped the tramp, and as the train began to snort, she threw out a hand and grabbed the rail and hauled herself up onto the step. The tramp made a last-ditch lunge, clawing after the girl, grabbing hold of her coat with a giant, filthy hand. She shrieked. Frederik didn't have time to think. He seized her arm and pulled her away from the old man's clutches and headlong into the carriage. The door smashed shut, knocking the tramp back onto the platform, sealing the girl and Frederik inside.

With a jolt and a shudder, the train began to move out of the station. A train they absolutely shouldn't be on.

"How wonderful," said the girl, clambering upright, disheveled and out of breath. "I saved your life and now you have saved mine! We are bound together *forever*."

And behind them on the receding platform, hand outstretched toward them still, the filthy tramp, his face livid and red, mouthed inaudible murder.

CHAPTER 5

The Lighthouse that Couldn't Possibly Be Either

Where are we heading?" Frederik fretted.

He didn't know where the train was going or where it had come from, nor what the tramp with the terrible breath had been hollering about, but he was certain he didn't like it. Any of it.

"Relax, rhubarb," said the weird girl, too tall, too big in the eyes, entirely too on the same train as Frederik.

"My name is *Sandwich*. Frederik *Sandwich*."

"I shall try to remember."

The shabby blue train rattled and shook like the earthquake that couldn't have possibly been, leaning lopsided

out of the bends and picking up speed. Scruffy bric-a-brac rolling stock, nobody on board, just Frederik and the weird girl. He had to get off. Next station. Soon as possible.

There were glimpses of underground arches, a burst of daylight, familiar landmarks, the church and the pub and the back of the mall. The weird girl was older than him, he decided, glancing at her whenever she looked away. What did she want from him? Normally nobody talked to him. Well, the next station would be Frederik's Gate, a matter of minutes. He'd hop off quick and run for school and never need to find out.

But the train shifted sideways. It rolled at an angle and pitched to the right, and he lost his balance. The main line curled away, beyond reach, and the train was heading in a new direction.

"Wrong way!" Frederik shouted and straightaway had no idea who he was shouting to. "This is wrong."

For the first time the girl looked worried too, gripping tight to a tarnished handrail Frederik couldn't reach. A clatter and a wobble and darkness again. The train angled downward into another tunnel. Gloomy archways, shifting shadows, odd things—wrong things. Broken crates and twisted metal, damp masonry, mossy and stained. For a moment, he thought he glimpsed a ghastly face staring back through the window. What had that tramp said? Zombies? He looked to his feet for reassurance, but at the end of his feet were hers.

"Who are you anyway?" he snapped.

"My name," she announced with solemnity, "is Pernille Yasemin Jensen. Adopted daughter of an upstanding upholsterer."

"Pernille," said Frederik. He pronounced it as she did, to rhyme with vanilla. "How interesting." Which frankly, it wasn't, given his rising panic. To mask it, he added, "I know that upholsterer's shop. It's at the end of my street."

"Correct," said Pernille Yasemin Jensen. "The very same. I followed you, in fact, to the station this morning. I watched you in the night, you see, from my bedroom window. You were gazing out from your own in the wake of the quake."

"You watched me?" he said, ever more uneasy. "You *followed* me?"

"I followed you, yes. To discuss the earthquake."

"It wasn't an earthquake."

"You see? We're discussing it already. How delightful."

They stood, swaying, in a short corridor.

"How long have you lived there?" he found himself asking. What he really meant was, *How long have you been watching me and following me around?*

"All my life," she said. "And all of yours." It wasn't at all what he wanted to hear.

"I've never noticed you before," he lied.

"Oh, but you have. Many times. You pretend to ignore me. Everyone does." She leaned in closer. Uncomfortably close. "Because I look different."

Frederik cleared his throat and glanced away. "That can't be true," he said, although it was.

Behind dusty glass there were seating compartments the length of the carriage. Ragged drapes at dirty windows. Drapes. On a train. And lamps on the walls, little sconces made to look like candles with comical conical shades. Orange. The lampshades were orange and the drapes were grubby beige.

"What kind of train has drapes?" he said to fill the awkward silence.

"I like it," said Pernille Yasemin Jensen. "It's chintzy."

"Trains should not be *chintzy*," he told her.

But his voice was drowned out by a banshee squeal, a scream of metal on metal, and he was thrown against the wall, banging his shoulder and bruising his ego and probably squashing the sandwiches in his backpack—curried herring and gazpacho, his mother's creation; she had been to a cooking class. And before he could react, his breath was squeezed out of him and a crushing weight pinned him to the wall and everything went utterly dark and woolly and smelled softly of cinnamon.

"Get off me," he managed. "Get off!" But he could hardly hear his own voice above the screech of the brakes and Pernille Yasemin Jensen on top of him, her long, white hair in his eyes and mouth. She tried to stand and he tried to help her, but then she was tipping and he was flailing, and both of them landed in a tangle on the floor, her leg on top of his head.

The lights flickered, died, and then blinked back on again. The train had stopped.

Frederik clambered up, stood on Pernille's hand, apologized profusely. He pressed his face to the dirty glass to find out where they were.

They were in a station. An old, abandoned wreck of a station, underground and dimly lit. Arched ceiling, tiled, much like the station at Frederik's Hill but dusty, deserted. Posters peeled from the walls, decades out of date, advertising drinks he had never heard of and ferry rides from the years before the bridge was built across the sea and the ferries were sent for scrap.

"Where are we?"

They had only traveled a matter of minutes, not even long enough to leave the municipal boundaries of Frederik's Hill. Somewhere above was somewhere near home, but he hadn't the slightest clue where.

"Municipal Hall," said Pernille. She leaned on his shoulder in a most unwelcome way, staring out and up. "And lighthouse."

"Please," said Frederik. "Be serious. Municipal Hall does not have a station and certainly not a *lighthouse*. Municipal Hall is miles and miles from the sea. My father works in Municipal Hall, and if there were a station or a lighthouse, he would surely have told me. It would be public knowledge."

But as he said it, his gaze drifted up to the tiles on the

ceiling in royal porcelain. Fine, blue letters on neglected white spelled along the length of the platform: *Frederik's Hill Municipal Hall and Lighthouse.*

"It's not a lighthouse," he murmured. "It can't possibly be."

Nothing moved out there. It looked as though nothing had moved out there for years. Dust coated the platform. Cobwebs dangled from dark corners. Stairs led up to a doorway, but the doors were boarded up. The place was a frozen snapshot of the past. Like some sinister museum.

He looked for a way to open the door. Couldn't find a handle. Was glad that he couldn't. Better by far to stay in here.

"Look," said Pernille. She was leaning through the sliding door to the seating compartment. "Look at this." She fingered the tatty drapes in the window—beige with thin, brown check and ragged tassels at the edges held behind loops of tarnished brass.

"What about them?" he asked.

She grabbed his sleeve and pressed his face to the glass. The platform was still, not a soul to be seen.

"The office," she said. "The same drapes!"

At the back of the platform, halfway along, between signs and broken seats, there was a door and a dirty window in the wall. The window was broken, a maze of cracks, no light. Behind the glass hung two tatty curtains of beige and thin, brown check.

"It's a mystery," she declared.

"It's curtain fabric," he told her. "Why wouldn't they reuse it? It's economical. This must be where the train is kept when it's not in use. I expect they bring it back into service when the newer ones are under maintenance. Perfectly sensible. We'll be away in a moment, heading back to Frederik's Hill. We'll jump off there and hopefully that dreadful tramp will be long gone."

Pernille pressed her shoulder against his until he was forced to give ground.

"Footprints," she whispered. "There, in the dust."

A single set of adult footprints, a workman's boot perhaps, led from the office door, turned to the left, and trailed away to the edge of the platform.

"Someone sleeps down here," she said. "Why else would they need drapes? They must have stolen them from the train to hide their hideaway."

"No," said Frederik. "If anyone uses that office, it would be the train driver. Or the station master."

"But this station isn't used. It doesn't need a station master. Those footprints must belong to some poor homeless person." Sudden horror washed across her face. "That tramp!"

"No," he insisted, more uneasy by the minute. "That would be absolutely against the rules. No one has been down here for years and years."

"These footprints are recent. Look at them! What is that hobo up to down here?" And then she gasped. "Underneath Her Ladyship's Municipal Hall. Under her very feet!"

Frederik's throat became unpleasantly tight. He looked the length of the carriage, couldn't see what lay beyond.

"He hates her," Pernille went on. "You heard him! A *monster*, he called her. Her Ladyship the Mayor!"

"Let's not read too much into this."

The disgusting diesel belched a cloud of fumes along the platform. The carriage jolted and began to move. The platform drifted by and they pitched suddenly into darkness.

"Thank goodness," he said. "We're on our way back to Frederik's Hill."

"No, nectarine dear. We're not going back. We are heading ever farther away."

She was right. They were. A terrible chill took hold of Frederik, as did an embarrassing urge to whimper. And the tramp's dire warning echoed in his head: *Don't ride that train. You don't know what's down there.*

CHAPTER 6

The Darkness

T he tatty old train jarred side to side in a pitch-black tunnel deep underground. Balance was impossible. Frederik took refuge in a threadbare seat, his shoulder braced against the wall. The lights flickered off and on again. They were going totally the wrong direction. School began in fifteen minutes. He was going to be in terrible trouble. If, of course, he lived.

Pernille tumbled into the opposite seat. She leaned across and pegged him with a single finger. "This is serious. It falls to you and I to foil that filthy man. So it's time we were fully introduced." She fixed her enormous eyes on his. "Don't you think?"

He looked around to see if there was a way out of the conversation. There was not.

"My name is Frederik," he said. "I told you that. Frederik Sandwich." The train clattered on, no sign of when or where it might stop.

"Sandwich, of course. It slipped my mind. A foreign name. And a handy lunchtime snack."

"I'm not foreign," he countered. "You're a lot more foreign than me."

"I hardly think so. Enumerate your heritage, if you would."

"My heritage?"

"Your parentage," she told him. "Your lineage, your ethnicity, your origins, your roots." She stared at him intently. She was a scary-looking girl. "Your ancestors are from elsewhere. I can tell from your name and your hair and your way of speaking."

"What's wrong with my hair?" he worried, trying to look up through the roof of his head and failing.

"Your hair is not blond, my little baguette. It is not linen fair like that of the lily-faced folk of Frederik's Hill. *My* hair, as you see, is ice white, from my maternal line. *Very* much local. From the tribes of Nordic adventurers who first settled this frosty region millennia ago."

"You still look weird," he said.

"Exotic, I'll grant you. My complexion, you see, is the olive of my father's bloodline. An Ottoman sultanate. Tahitian elders. Of that I am all but certain. Meanwhile *your* hair is a rather wishy-washy brown. And you speak, I have noticed, with a hint of an overseas accent. So from where do they come, your peculiar hair and pronunciation?"

"From my parents," he said begrudgingly. "They're not from this country, that's true. But I am. I am from Frederik's Hill. And Frederik's Hill is exactly where I'm going just as soon as I get off this train!"

Pernille nodded slowly and a smile oozed across her face. "As I suspected. Not only are we in one another's debt, but we are also, you might say, of one kind. Immigrants. Outsiders."

"I am not an outsider."

"Really? And yet the local children do not allow you into their local conversations."

He tensed, embarrassed. Why did she have to see that? Say that? "They misunderstand."

"*Do* they?"

"Because of my name. I think. Or maybe I do have a touch of an accent. But I was born on Frederik's Hill, in Frederik's Hospital, at the end of Frederik's Street. I belong here. I follow the rules like everyone else. If one follows the rules and expectations, one is quickly accepted."

"And how's that going for you?"

"Well," he said. "It's… Well. The thing is… Well, I'm sure I *will* belong sometime soon. It's just a matter of time."

She smoothed her sleeves with the palms of her hands for no practical reason. Tossed her hair back regally. She placed a hand on his arm and leaned in horribly close. "They shun you, don't they?" All he could see were her eyes and a spray of freckles. "They shun you because of your foreign name and your funny enunciation."

"I'm not funny," he insisted. "Or *foreign*. I was born here."

"As was I, but that makes little difference. What matters on Frederik's Hill is looking and talking and acting exactly like everyone else. And I mean *exactly*."

"But that's a good thing. That's as it should be. It's orderly. It's predictable."

"It's prejudice," said Pernille and patted his hand. "And well you know it, my friend."

"I'm not your friend." He was flustered now. "You're a girl, and I hardly know you."

"But still, we are bound by common experience. By our cruel isolation. And now by the lifelong debt I owe you, having snatched your knuckle head from the path of the seven twenty-two train."

Frederik opened his mouth to say something, couldn't think of anything, closed it again. Could that be right?

Without warning, the brakes screeched all over again. Pernille was tossed from her seat and slid across the floor. Frederik ended up wedged in a corner on top of his backpack, his sandwiches surely beyond rescue. The darkness broke.

In the window, their own reflected faces gave way to an open space of marble and pillars and chandeliers. A cavernous space, partly lit, but no one to be seen. Desolate platforms reaching back. A staircase sweeping up and out of sight. Iron benches under arches. Everything wrought in decorative flourishes. A railway station from another century, large enough and grand enough for hundreds of passengers, all at once. Many hundreds—an army.

The train complained to a halt.

"Where are we now?" he asked. "Let's get off quick! Find an adult and tell them about that tramp."

Pernille pulled herself up at the nearest door. Rattled the handle. "Still locked."

A marble shield on the wall. Lots of them. A single initial on each. *F*, for Frederik. And Frederik recognized it right away. He had seen it many times: on the doors of the pubs, in supermarkets, on beer bottles in Father's hand, on the archways of an enormous building at the far corner of King Frederik's Garden Park.

"The brewery."

Pernille gave a perky little jump. "Do you think?"

"It must be. We came from the mainline to Municipal Hall. What's next if you carry on in that direction? The eastern edge of the Garden Park, the skating rink with the hot dog cart, and then the brewery."

"That's odd," said Pernille. "I didn't know it had a station."

"No," he said, feeling suddenly cold again. "It doesn't."

He stared out at the stillness. Knew beyond doubt that he shouldn't be here. He *had* to find a way off the train and back to the surface. He reached for his backpack but was interrupted by the sudden sensation of flying sideways and colliding with the wall. They were off again, building speed. Pernille stepped on his ankle. Failed to apologize. She gripped the handrail he couldn't reach and somehow stayed upright. The brewery disappeared, and the train roared into darkness. This was a nightmare. The railway had to be off-limits. It didn't *exist*. If they were expected to know it existed, someone would have mentioned it. Wouldn't they? He resolved to sit down and avoid learning anything more that he wasn't supposed to know. But just as he reached the seat, his eardrums were assaulted once more and the train was stopping as abruptly as it had started. Down he went all over again, all over the floor, all over Pernille's sneakers.

The train hissed to a halt.

"Now wherever are we?" asked Pernille.

Bruised and forlorn, he crossed the compartment on hands and knees, pulled himself up to the glass again.

Everything out there was brown and rank, liquid dripping all over a filthy platform. Valves and pipes climbed the wall in tangles. Knuckles and faucets and welded joints, an ancient spaghetti of plumbing. A moist, unpleasant smell. He shuddered.

Swinging in the diesel draught, a discolored piece of tin suspended from a chain announced *The Cisterns*.

"What cisterns?" he asked. Condensation dribbled from black brickwork and pooled in dark puddles. He thought he caught a movement in the shadows. *You don't know what's down there*, the tramp had said. He scanned the gloom in panic, but then he was tumbling again. The train lurched away from the horrid, sodden station. The lights went out. Absolute blackness. The clamor of wheels against rails and the sensation of all his innards being slopped to one side.

"Aaaagh," he said.

In the window, there was nothing but darkness and his own scared face.

Then dim light.

"Another station!" Pernille exclaimed. "Well, I think it's a station."

The train had slowed under an arched ceiling of dry, red brick. There was no platform as such, but instead, a wooden loading bay. A deck of sturdy timber, covered in straw and sawdust. Also, if he wasn't mistaken, gigantic piles of dried-up animal dung. The deck had only one exit.

A huge brick arch, the height of four men, leading into a shadowy passageway. There was an enormous gate. Heavy iron bars.

"A prison," said Pernille. "It's a prison. For giants."

"Not giants," said Frederik, for he had pieced it together, mapping out the route in his mind even before he spotted the notice. They were looping the fringe of King Frederik's Garden Park, and now they had to be somewhere beneath the zoo. Sure enough, away to their left, a plank of wood was nailed to the bare brick wall. Hand-painted letters: *Elephant House.*

"It's a station for elephants," he said, aware of how preposterous he sounded.

"This railway connects every important building on Frederik's Hill," Pernille breathed. "And no one knows, except for that tramp! What can he be up to? What evils? It frightens me, fruitcake. We are all alone down here. All *alone.*"

"Ahem." Somebody cleared their throat.

Frederik sat upright with a jolt and a hammering heart. Pernille too.

Standing between the seats, staring down at them, was a woman.

A woman in a dark-blue uniform. Straight skirt, sensible shoes, a blazer, and a hat—a hat with a peak and a silver badge.

She looked at Frederik. And also at Pernille. Her left eye, unless he was imagining it, pointed a different direction to the right.

The train went nowhere at all.

The woman pulled out a pocket watch, examined it, frowned, and then in a croaky voice, as though out of practice, said, "Tickets, please."

CHAPTER 7

A M!sdemeanor

Y our tickets," the woman repeated solemnly. "Please."

"Well," said Pernille. "Here's the thing, you see…"

Frederik grabbed at his pocket. "Here's my annual rail pass," he said, and he waved it in the air.

The conductor aimed one eye at the rail pass and another elsewhere. Her contempt was clear, even if her focal point was less so. "Not valid on this line," she said.

Frederik, panicking, scrutinized the small print on the back of the pass. It was very small indeed, and there was an awful lot of it. "Which line are we on?"

"Which line? The Frederik's Hill Municipal Branch Line! Do they teach you children nothing?"

Frederik looked at the pass. Then Pernille. Then the conductor. "There isn't a Frederik's Hill Municipal Branch Line," he said.

The conductor glanced pointedly out of the window at the abandoned platform, then pointedly back at Frederik. "I beg to differ."

A fuzzy fog inserted itself between Frederik's ears. He couldn't think. "We didn't mean to get on this train," he said. "It was an accident."

"Accident?"

"Well, no. Not an accident. We were being chased! Pursued by a seething madman. A filthy old tramp with terrible breath. He was going to kill us. In a very unpleasant way. We had no choice but get on the train. We were running for our lives!"

The conductor blinked. Twice. "I've heard them all, dear. All the excuses."

"It's not an excuse!" Pernille insisted. "We were escaping mortal peril. In fear of a gory demise in front of one hundred commuters."

"*Were* you?" the conductor said, raising a single

eyebrow. It seemed to Frederik this was a look she had practiced for just such circumstances.

"Yes," said Pernille. "And there, you see, is our, shall we call it, *dilemma*."

"I see," said the conductor, nodding. "But where is your, shall we call it, *ticket*?"

Frederik was feeling nauseous. He had broken the *law* now. And he'd been caught!

Pernille pressed her hands together as though in prayer. "We don't exactly have, you see, *tickets*, exactly. The Frederik's Hill station, you see, as far as we were able to gather, does not sell tickets for this particular train."

"You are correct," said the conductor. The lights in the carriage all went off. For a second, Frederik was tempted to run, but he couldn't see a thing. And then they flickered back on again, and his chance was gone.

"The stations do not sell tickets for this train, and neither does anywhere else," the conductor explained. "The sale of tickets for the Frederik's Hill Municipal Branch Line is prohibited by the borough and has been for more than a quarter century." She cleared her throat. "Now. Once again. May I see your tickets, please?"

They stared back, bewildered.

"How," said Frederik, doing his utmost to be very polite indeed, "if you please, madam, does one buy a ticket? Could one purchase a ticket directly from you, perhaps?"

The conductor regarded him as she might a piece of old gum stuck to the seat of one of her carriages. "No."

He listened to the buzz in his head and it didn't help at all. "We're innocent! That tramp is the one you ought to be talking to. He's up to no good. He has a lair! A hideaway hideout hidden deep in the depths of your branch line. He's a horrible homeless hobo of the very worst kind!"

"Please!" The conductor was losing patience. "Thirty-five years I have worked this line, and that is the most fanciful story I have heard yet."

"We saw his footprints," Pernille explained. "He has infiltrated your stations!"

"Enough!" The conductor peered at them both simultaneously from under the peak of her cap. "Traveling without a ticket is a misdemeanor contrary to the Municipal Transportation Bylaw of 1937, section eleven, subsection two. I regret, my dears, that I shall be forced to report you."

All trace of saliva abandoned Frederik's mouth. He was going to be reported. For a misdemeanor!

Pernille gathered herself as tall as she could given that she was sitting down. She folded her hands primly in front of herself. "Do you know who I am?" she inquired.

The conductor squinted. "No."

"Evidently."

The conductor produced a notepad from her pocket. A pencil. She licked the end of the pencil. Winced. "Then why don't you tell me, dear. Your names, please?"

"You don't recognize me?" Pernille tossed her long, white hair. It didn't entirely work.

"Your *names*," said the conductor with rather more emphasis.

Pernille hesitated, opened her mouth, closed it. Looked to the ceiling and rolled her eyes. "Muriel," she said.

Frederik choked. Tried to make it sound like a cough. Watched the conductor's pencil scratch across the notepad.

"Muriel what?"

"Muriel Kristensen."

"Kristensen?"

"Like Her Ladyship the Mayor," said Pernille, lying with impressive fluency.

"As a matter of fact," the conductor scowled, "I do *not* like her. And your name, young man?"

Frederik tried to make sound come out, but all he managed was a kind of croak.

"His name is Eduardo," Pernille put in. "Eduardo Esteban de Enchilada."

The conductor eyed her carefully. "Are you sure?"

"Perfectly sure," said Pernille.

"Foreign, is he?"

"Of course he is. Just listen to him."

Frederik opened his mouth to protest but couldn't think what to say.

"*Enchilada* like the lunchtime snack?"

"Yes."

The conductor's pen scrawled slowly over the page.

"The rules and regulations of the Frederik's Hill Municipal Branch Line are unambiguous on the topic of tickets," the conductor explained. "Tickets are *required*. At all times. No exceptions. No excuses."

She strode to the door. She pulled the window down,

put a whistle to her lips, and let loose a terrific blast that made Frederik's ears ring. The old blue train lurched, stopped, lurched again, and then gradually gathered speed, leaving the dilapidated elephant house behind and plunging them back into blackness.

"A summons will be issued," the conductor announced. "Sentence passed, fines levied, that sort of thing."

"When?" Frederik managed. They had given false names. Wasn't that a crime too? Or might that somehow save them?

"Soon. Forthwith. By return of post. I don't know exactly. It's not my department."

"Let's hope it's not the mayor's department," Pernille said. "For your sake. Her Ladyship will not be pleased to find you have detained, well, let's just say her most loyal voter-to-be. Still less when she hears you are harboring a tramp under her own Municipal Hall!"

The conductor fixed Pernille with a steely stare. "Don't talk to me about your precious mayor. I have served this borough longer than she has. And let me assure you that woman hears no one. Least of all foreign children."

The train clattered and rattled. Frederik gripped the

seat in an effort not to slide off. The conductor stayed standing, unsupported, flexing her knees and riding the bumps and rolls as though they were nothing.

"How dare you say that about Her Ladyship?" Pernille spat. "The mayor is very tolerant. She welcomes all with open arms. She is hosting an international festival! The nations of the world will converge on Frederik's Hill. A celebration of diversity."

"A celebration of the mayor, more like. She only cares about herself. My branch line was once the jewel of the transportation system. Look at her now!" She spread her arms wide. "Neglected, dejected, and whose fault is that? Who closed the stations? Who cut the budget? Mayor Kristensen! This line has not been maintained for decades. Our locomotive is in a terrible state. And the tracks and carriages? My goodness! Only last night we were almost derailed. Shook like a roller coaster for nearly a mile. It's a wonder we didn't wake half the borough!"

A light outside. The brakes screeched. Everything rattled and juddered.

A sudden reminder.

"The earthquake," Frederik gasped. "In the night."

A narrow platform slid into view. Coated with fine, white dust, mouse droppings here and there. The walls were tiled from floor to ceiling. Enormous floral patterns: blue on white. As familiar to Frederik as his own home. And for very good reason. Frederik's home was the end of an outstretched arm of what had once been the Royal Porcelain Factory. One of the factory's chimney stacks rose to the sky right outside his bedroom window. These blue designs on shining white were the Royal Porcelain Factory's hallmark. This station was part of the factory. Had to be. And somewhere above their heads was Frederik's house! He knew every block and building of the factory—from the outside, anyway. It had closed some years ago, production moved elsewhere. The buildings were being converted into homes, but whole wings remained abandoned and boarded up. There were boys who claimed to have been inside. He had never heard them mention a railway. Of course, they didn't actually talk to him. But he did his best to eavesdrop from a distance and never once had he heard of a train. Yet here it was. Right under their feet. Right under his house.

"Of course!" he said. "The shaking! Last night! It *did* wake half the borough!"

The conductor looked guiltily from side to side. Cleared her throat. "I don't know what you're talking about."

"You do!"

"I do not."

"It was this train!" Frederik was on his feet now, all excited, his words emerging in little panting breaths. "I knew it! It wasn't an earthquake at all. It was this crumbling railway. You said so yourself!"

"Simmer down, dear."

"We must inform the mayor," said Pernille, ice in her voice.

The conductor turned urgently toward her. "The mayor? No, dear. Don't do that." A nervous tic had developed under one eye. "She'd misunderstand."

"Misunderstand what? You are involved, aren't you? You and that tramp!"

"I don't know any tramp."

"What are the two of you plotting? Something malicious. He said he knew all about the earthquake. That only he knew. You and that vagrant have rigged this train to cause earthquakes. That's it, isn't it? You're going to shake the town to pieces. And blame Her Ladyship!"

The conductor watched Pernille nervously. "You're much mistaken, my dear."

"Then why can't I tell her? What's the big secret? You work for her, don't you? Or do you, in fact, work *against* her?"

The conductor shifted from foot to foot. "May I point out it is you two who are traveling without tickets!" She leaned toward Frederik. "Remind me of your name, dear. I'm a little forgetful."

"Frederik Sandwich," he said.

Her eyebrows bounced upward. She whipped her notebook from her pocket. "Not *Eduardo*?"

"Oh," he said and flushed a vivid purple.

Pernille scowled at him.

The conductor crossed out her notes and made the correction. "*Frederik Sandwich.* I'm glad we cleared that up. And we shall add a second charge: misleading a borough official."

The train was moving again. The Royal Porcelain Factory slipped away. Everything out there was gloom, and he felt sick and small and tired. He wanted out. He wanted daylight. He was appallingly late for school. He was going to miss science altogether. And sooner or later, a summons would come and he would go to prison, or worse—a home for delinquent boys with foreign names.

"And is *your* name falsified, young lady?" the conductor asked. "Muriel, was it?"

But Pernille didn't reply, and then Frederik's eyes were smarting with sudden sunshine. The train burst from the dark. Familiar track! There was the church and there was the hospital, and dead ahead the next tunnel, dipping down to where they'd begun. Frederik's Hill! Exactly where they had boarded. Commuters and shoppers and parents with babies drew back from the noise, and all along the length of the train, with a deafening crash, the doors of the old blue train burst open again.

Pernille grabbed his hand and was running. He fell off the seat. Found his feet. Sprinted after her, dragging his backpack, and toppled, listless, out of the carriage. People eyed them both with grave suspicion. But there was no tramp. The platform was steady underfoot. It was any old Friday morning on Frederik's Hill. There was nothing out of place or out of the ordinary except for them.

They ran for the stairs. Fled the station. Caught their breath in chilly sunshine in the center of the square.

"We made it," said Pernille. "We're safe!"

"She took my name!" said Frederik.

"Don't worry. Her career is finished. I'm taking this to the top. Shall we skip school today?"

"No!" said Frederik, clutching his backpack and moving away from her as quickly as he could. "No, we absolutely shan't. You've got me into enough trouble already!"

CHAPTER 8

S!lence

The school hallway was long and deserted. Every inch of it squealed underfoot like an alarm. He tiptoed past each closed door. There was murmuring behind the walls. Through hazy glass, he saw rows of heads, out of focus.

Never had he been so catastrophically late for class. Lateness was for surly, unruly boys with gum and bad manners and feeble minds. But afraid of further mishaps, he'd abandoned the trains and taken the bus, and it took forever. The first lessons of the day were over, recess too, and it was more than halfway to lunchtime as he tiptoed guiltily toward his classroom.

The door was closed like all the others.

No sound.

He wondered if he should knock. This was a completely unfamiliar situation. Frederik took his education seriously, sensibly, followed all the rules. Arrived early, paid attention, turned his homework in on time. He did not take rides on forbidden trains in the wrong direction without a ticket and end up caught and late for school! It wasn't his fault, he kept telling himself. He'd been fleeing from a crazy tramp. He *had* to tell someone about the crazy tramp. And the train conductor. Was Pernille right? Was the earthquake a plot to discredit the mayor?

Distracted and distressed, he opened the door a tad too quickly.

He found himself face-to-face with faces. Upturned, mouth-open faces. An entire classroom of faces and weighted, bated silence.

"Frederik Sandwich?" said Miss Moesby, midway through a mathematical conundrum. One of Miss Moesby's eyes grew rather wide and the other seemed to shrink. "Explain yourself!"

His throat closed tight. He blinked. Too many times.

Classmates stared without pity, willing unwell upon him. He opened his mouth but failed to produce any sound. He should have rehearsed his explanation.

"I'm terribly sorry I'm late. I got on a train."

"A train?"

"The wrong train. By mistake."

Snickers and mockery.

"There was a tramp!" he tried to explain. "A dangerous madman!"

The spiteful laughter of twenty-five twelve-year-olds.

"Be quiet!" the teacher shouted.

What could he say? He wasn't explaining. "The earthquake! It wasn't an earthquake at all!"

And then he decided to shut up. Because Miss Moesby had opened a single eye as wide as a single eye could be, while the other dwindled to a puckered pinhole.

His classmates watched his every move like predators.

"Have I *not*," inquired Miss Moesby, "been *clear* on this *topic*?"

A couple of heads dared a nod. His own desk, in the front row, yawned empty. Sitting close to the teacher no longer seemed like such a great arrangement.

"I wasn't here," he said. "I'm so sorry."

Twenty-five pairs of eyes flitted from Frederik to Miss Moesby and back again.

Frederik, entirely unpracticed at being in trouble, blundered on as best he could. "I can explain the whole thing. The earthquake. Everyone is talking about it."

Miss Moesby bent forward till her eye was level with his. "*We*," she said, in a tone he had never heard her use before, "are *not*."

"Talking about it?"

"*Not* talking about it."

"Why not?"

"Do I *need*," Miss Moesby breathed in his face, "to explain *again*?"

He nodded overeagerly. "If you wouldn't mind. I wasn't here the first time, you see."

She drew herself up to her full height and looked down at the top of his head. "There has been no *earthquake*," she bellowed. "No shaking, no shuddering. *None*." She let the announcement ring around the walls and die away in the rafters. Nobody moved. Nobody had ever heard her bellow before.

"But that tremor in the night," Frederik said.

Her nose swooped toward his till they virtually touched. "The *principal*," she hissed, "has *prohibited*"—her breath smelled of soap—"*mention*, of this ridiculous *rumor*! Any child who disobeys will find themselves in *detention*! Starting, Frederik Sandwich, with you!"

His stomach dropped like a little avalanche.

"Report after school to the principal's office, and let this be a lesson to one and all. This topic"—she rolled her head back and bared a set of pointy little teeth—"is forever *closed*."

Detention? Frederik mouthed, appalled.

He found his seat and curled as small as he could. He wanted the chair to swallow him. Erik the Awkward and Erica Engel whispered and flicked things at him. A soggy wad of chewed paper hit him on the head and hopped across his desk. He twisted, angry. "Stop that!"

Erik the Awkward, two rows back, grinned malevolently. Erica Engel, directly behind him, doubled over with laughter.

He tried to focus. Had no idea what Miss Moesby was talking about. Couldn't catch her thread.

A detention. She'd given him a detention! And for what? For mentioning what all of them must have felt?

There *had* been shaking in the night. And he knew why! The mayor was under attack. The whole borough! So why weren't they allowed to talk about it? It didn't make sense! His thoughts swirled in a kind of storm. If he knew what the earthquake really was, surely he should be thanked? Rewarded? Forgiven his ticketing misdemeanor?

Miss Moesby turned her back.

Hands grabbed the back of his seat and started wobbling it violently.

"What's that, Flipper-lick?" Erik the Awkward whispered. "An earthquake!"

Erica Engel burst out laughing, spraying spit all over his shoulder. "An *earthquake*!"

"What did I tell you?" And from nowhere, Miss Moesby was upon them, hand slapping down on Erica's desk.

"Nothing, miss," said Erica, reddening. "It was him. Frederik Sandwich."

"No, it wasn't!" Frederik wailed.

"I warned you there would be repercussions!" Miss Moesby yelled. "You, you, and *you*!" She pointed pointedly at Erica Engel, Erik the Awkward, and Frederik. "*Double* detention! One full hour! With the principal!"

A chilly silence descended on the room. Just the sound of pencils. Twenty-five extremely focused students.

Frederik burned with confusion and shame. Double detention! What were his parents going to say? They insisted on him following rules, fitting in. Now he'd be grounded, confined to his room, allowance withheld forever. Any hope of replacing the shattered telescope would be gone.

And yet the telescope was proof there had been shaking! Physical evidence in pieces all over his bedroom floor! Why would anyone pretend it didn't happen? The teachers? The principal, of all people? How could he raise the alarm if he wasn't allowed to mention it?

His day limped by like an agony. No one would meet his eye. He smoldered with guilt, squirmed with the worry of all he knew and couldn't reveal. What if the mayor was in actual danger? Wouldn't it be his fault if he didn't let someone know?

No one mentioned the earthquake. No one breathed a word—not at lunchtime, not in the hallways, certainly not in the classroom. He didn't understand, and he still didn't as he shuffled red-faced out of class, banged and barged into by the others, and instead of following them into the afternoon, he turned right through an archway to the dark door of the principal's office.

He had never in all his schooling been inside.

Heart in his throat, he gave a single knock.

"Enter." A voice like needles.

A large, round table.

Mrs. Madsen, a woman of spiky edges, all nose and elbows, was silhouetted against a window.

"Don't just stand there," she hissed. "Sit down next to the others."

There was only one. Benny Bjornesen. A brawler from the year above him. Frederik had always kept a safe distance from Benny. There were stories. He chose a chair as far away as he could. But now there were footsteps. The door was flung wide. Erica Engel. Erik the Awkward. They glared at him. They blamed him. They took their seats in sullen silence.

No one spoke.

Mrs. Madsen's seat creaked beneath her spiky behind.

A clock on the wall ticktocked.

Slowly.

"You all know why you're here," said Mrs. Madsen.

It made Frederik jump.

She fixed her gaze on Erik the Awkward. "Yes?"

Erik the Awkward narrowed his eyes toward Frederik. "I know why I'm here, miss," he muttered.

"And you?" Mrs. Madsen turned her attention to Benny Bjornesen.

Benny, notoriously slow on the uptake, nodded his head, eyes on the table. "Talking about the—" And then he stopped.

"The what?"

"The *earthquake*!" It erupted out of Frederik's mouth like a torpedo.

Benny Bjornesen, Erik the Awkward, and Erica Engel stopped breathing. Entirely.

The clock ticked.

There was a very long pause.

The clock tocked.

Mrs. Madsen twisted her spindly fingers together.

Her eyes were glacier cold.

Her mouth was a tight little line.

"Sorry," he murmured.

"*Are* you?" she wondered.

"I shouldn't have said that."

"No. You shouldn't."

"It won't happen again."

"You're right about that."

He sat there. In silence. A great big lump in his throat. Afraid of all of them, avoiding their eyes, through sixty minutes of sorry soul-searching.

When Mrs. Madsen finally released them with a last rebuke and a lick of her insect lips, Frederik let the others hurry away, heads down. Then, heart in mouth, he waited for Mrs. Madsen to notice he was still there.

"What now?" she demanded.

"I'm sorry," he said. "I really am. But there's something you should know."

He tried to find the words. A train. No, better not mention the train. He was in enough trouble with that already. The tramp then. Yes. The tramp underneath Municipal Hall. Except no. He couldn't reveal he'd been down there, could he? What was he going to say?

"On the contrary," she said. "There is something *you* should know." She loomed closer. "The borough is preparing to be in the spotlight. Do you understand? An international festival. These rumors of earthquakes are a scam, a plot to undermine us. The work of insidious immigrants, no doubt."

"There *is* a plot," Frederik yelped. "You're right! But it isn't immigrants. I know all about it!"

"What do you know, Frederik Sandwich?" the principal demanded. "And why? Ah, of course. Your family is foreign."

"No. They aren't. Not exactly. Not anymore."

"Are you involved in this plot? Are they?"

He tried to back away but was pinned against the wall.

"Do you know more than you are telling me?"

"Yes," he said. "No. Well, not exactly."

"If I found any pupil of my school to be blackening the name of Frederik's Hill, let me assure you, there would be profound consequences. Firm, final, fitting consequences. For him and his family! Is that clear?"

Frederik made for the door, breathless. His *family*? Now he'd got his family in trouble?

"And don't let me hear your name again," she snarled at his back. "After all, it isn't a name I'll be likely to forget."

CHAPTER 9

The Ramasubramanian Superstore

S ausage!" A shrill voice. Loud. From the other side of
the street. "Sausage!"

Frederik had almost made it home. Almost.
On and off the train unscathed. No unexpected detours into
darkness. Rail pass accepted as normal, not so much as a
second glance. Out of the station and up the steps. Across
the square, past the library, down the side street, into the
shadow of Municipal Hall, glancing up at the clock tower
that actually might be a lighthouse, though it didn't make
any sense. He had reached the shabby convenience store no
more than three or four minutes from home.

And then she caught him.

"Strawberry!"

"*Sandwich!*" he flung back in irritation.

"Precisely!" And there she was, long and gangly, hair that didn't match her anything else. Striding across the road without regard for oncoming traffic.

"Go away!"

"Why would I do that?"

"Because!"

It wasn't any kind of answer, but the truth was he didn't have an answer. Just a concrete conviction that Pernille Yasemin Jensen had caused enough trouble already. He tried to dart away. But at just the wrong moment, from the shade of the shop doorway stepped a shabby little man with skin even darker than hers. The keeper of the corner shop. Everyone knew who he was. Nobody talked to him.

"Young man!" he said with a conspicuous accent, opening his stubby arms and preventing Frederik from getting by. "How fortuitous! I have candy bars at half price today. Very good value. Only lightly dented. Earthquake damage special offer."

Frederik had been about to squeeze by and run, but now he stopped. Dead.

"Earthquake? Did you say *earthquake*?"

The little man smiled, but an edge of uncertainty crept upon him now.

"There *was* an earthquake, wasn't there?" Frederik said. "Well, not an earthquake, but shaking!" Hope leaped in his chest. At last! An adult who agreed it had happened!

"Chocolate?" said the shopkeeper. "Dark, milk, or however you like it. Wrappers only slightly ripped. The Ramasubramanian Superstore will cater to your every boyish whim. Please step inside."

"Ripped by all the shaking in the night?" Frederik stepped to the doorway, peering inside. He couldn't see much—racks of faded boxes and bedraggled publications.

The shopkeeper tried to usher him through the door. "Very little damage," he said. "Hardly a scratch. Earthquake? Nonsense. Forget I mentioned it. Half-price soda, half-price cakes."

And then Pernille was upon him, gabbling and distracting him. "My little grapefruit. I've been looking for you ever since school. Where did you get to? We have sinister secrets to expose!"

"There *was* shaking," Frederik told her. "I *knew* there was. And this man says so!"

"Of course there was."

"But people won't talk about it! Nobody! Not even at school. Not even the principal. I don't know why. She said something about the international festival."

Pernille gasped. "The festival?" She raised her fingers to her face. "The festival is the most important event of Her Ladyship's term of office. It's going to be huge. They say she might restore the fabled fountains of Frederik the Tenth. The tramp and that criminal conductor must be planning to sabotage it—with an earthquake! We must go to the mayor immediately. Municipal Hall is just across the street."

"No," he hissed. "Not there. They have my name. My family will get into trouble. My father works in Municipal Hall. My mother works at the library. They'll get fired. Fined. Deported! What if my family gets deported? I'd be all on my own—in a prison for delinquent boys with unusual names."

Pernille regarded him earnestly from her somewhat greater height. "You will always have me," she said. "We are indebted to each other forever."

"Good grief. I don't think you understand the trouble you have landed me in!"

"Me?"

"You!"

"I didn't cause the earthquake."

"It wasn't an earthquake!"

"Oh yes it was," said the shabby shopkeeper. "A most terrible earthquake of unprecedented proportions. I awoke in the dead of the dark to a crescendo, as though the whole building had been picked up and rattled. Cans and bottles raining onto the floor. My stock smashing and crashing and rolling around. Like an explosion that wouldn't let up. The whole hill, the whole city, shaken and toppled and tipped on its side, goods worth thousands of crowns completely ruined, broken glass everywhere, sticky, fizzing puddles. All my cartons warping in a sea of spilled milk."

Frederik and Pernille, side by side, stared at the shopkeeper, somewhat dumbfounded.

"Tell me, dear man," said Pernille. "Has anyone asked you to keep this earthquake quiet?"

"Quiet? It was deafening. Cacophonous! When at last it stopped and I was able to safely descend the stairs, I stood and stared at the wreckage for half an hour, ankle deep in a mess of rice and lemonade. I simply did not know what to do next."

Frederik ventured into the store. He couldn't fight it. Had to see.

Few people frequented the Ramasubramanian Superstore, and was it any surprise? What kind of a name was *Ramasubramanian*? Ridiculous. If you wanted to trade on Frederik's Hill, the very first thing you did was name your business *Frederik's*. The cramped little space was crammed with rickety racks and sagging shelves. Cartons of cereal, warped. Fruit and vegetables, far from fresh. The shop was in sharp contrast with the rest of the street. Neighboring stores sold sushi and mohair and pearls and high-end gadgets. There were upmarket shoe shops, chic boutiques. The Ramasubramanian Superstore seemed to be aimed at a different class of customer entirely. And it smelled of a sickly mix of soup and detergent and spices. The floor was sticky. The little man had evidently not mopped the damage up very thoroughly.

But damage there had clearly been.

The shopkeeper followed Frederik into the store at

alarmingly close quarters. They were roughly the same height. Pernille peered down over the top of the shopkeeper's head.

"We think we know what caused the shaking," Frederik told the little man.

"Ganesh." The shopkeeper nodded.

"Bless you," Pernille said and offered a crumpled tissue.

"The *lord* Ganesh," the shopkeeper clarified. "My dear mother, sadly departed, told me to expect it. I should have listened. I am a little hazy on the details. But she assured me that one day Ganesh, Remover of Obstacles, would sweep away all impediments to my path. And I felt in the dead of the night that this shaking might be that moment. It was, I dared to hope, Ganesh, as my mother predicted. He takes the form of an elephant, you see."

"An elephant?" said Frederik.

"What else could cause such an earthquake after dark if not an elephant?"

Pernille twisted a long strand of silver-white hair into a knot and sucked it for several seconds. "I can think of one or two alternatives."

"My mother was adamant," the shopkeeper assured her. "This has all the hallmarks of Ganesh. It is his MO."

"It was a train," said Frederik emphatically. "An underground train."

"A train?" The shopkeeper laughed. "What a silly idea, child. Your head is full of fluff."

"It *was* a train. It really was. Why will no one understand?"

"Having a party, Flipper-wreck?" A voice from the doorway. Familiar faces. Peering inside. Sneering. Erica Engel. Erik the Awkward. "Found your own people at last? Isn't that nice. All the foreigners together." The two of them strode away, their low laughter hanging in the air.

"No!" Frederik called after them. "I'm from here!"

"Now those, my dear dill pickle," said Pernille, "are actual half-wits, in case you were wondering."

"They've got it all wrong," he retorted. "I am not foreign. You're not my people. Either of you! I was born here. I belong!"

The shopkeeper eyed Frederik darkly. "You are ignorant enough to be a local, it seems to me."

Frederik, angry and embarrassed, failed to keep hold of his tongue. "If you don't like it here," he said, "why don't you go back where you belong?"

The shopkeeper's eyes locked on to his. Evident anger.

But worse than that, a sadness. An overwhelming sadness. Frederik was instantly ashamed of himself. Mortified. What an awful thing to say. Pernille too glared at him in shock and disappointment. Why had he said that? It was the kind of thing the nasty neighbors said to him, and he hated it.

The shopkeeper's face fell toward the floor. He closed his eyes. "If only I *could* go back," he breathed. "Ever since I came to this terrible place, my life is a catastrophe." He paced the sticky floor in dirty slippers. "I built the Ramasubramanian Superstore with my bare hands, I, Venkatamahesh Ramasubramanian. I stock everything a person could possibly want—cans and jars and gum and cigars, and all within a sensible budget. Modest wares at modest prices. It is a lesson my father passed along to me before passing on. I have held it dear to my heart, first in my father's store on a dusty street in the warm land of my home, and now here, in a store of my own at the end of a terribly long sea voyage in the far, frosty north of another continent entirely. I had a dream, you see—a chain of stores, offering reasonable choice at a reasonable price. What could possibly be wrong with such a plan?"

"You seem a little short of customers," Pernille suggested gently.

"I have tried to lure them in! With banners and offers that nobody could refuse. They have refused! I have sold virtually nothing in months. I have watched my goods slip one item at a time beyond their sell-by date. Always waiting, every day, waiting for customers. But do they come? No, they do not! And yet there are people, goodness yes, plenty of people passing by. Tall, haughty, blond-haired people, with expensive coats, on expensive bicycles, off to buy luxuries. Finest Darjeeling from Frederik's Teas, fancy patisserie from Frederik's Breadsticks. The folk of Frederik's Hill like their luxuries, you see. And they like their luxuries local, their shopkeepers tall and blond, like themselves. They do not value value!"

"It has nothing to do with value," Pernille sighed. "That's not why they stay away. The people of Frederik's Hill are snobs. Preening, prejudiced snobs."

The shopkeeper regarded her with sudden respect. "Exactly," he said. "Like those obnoxious kids." He whirled on Frederik. "Like you!"

Frederik backed toward the open door, deeply ashamed, deeply humiliated. "I had better go."

"Please do," said the shopkeeper. "I will sell my slightly dented chocolate to someone more deserving."

Frederik stepped off the step and into the rush of the rush hour. Bicycles fizzing by in their hundreds. Buses lurching. The lights of Municipal Hall shining out over all of Frederik's Hill. His family had come here full of hope, before he was born, to build a new life. And now, in a single turbulent night and day, it all seemed awfully insecure. And was it *his* fault? No. He hadn't meant to say what he said. He hadn't meant to upset anyone. But he seemed to have caused a whole pile of problems anyway.

Well, he would fix it. He would fix it now. And he would start where he ought to have started all along—with grown-ups. Sensible, responsible grown-ups. His own mother and father.

CHAPTER 10

Derailed

He jogged around the bend and past the upholsterer's window. The upholsterer's shop was a chaos of benches, furniture pulled apart. Tall men with tools and rolls of fabric. He must have walked by a thousand times, two thousand, ten thousand. Never paid it a moment's attention. The ground level was glass and salmon-pink plaster. The windows reflected the traffic. A peculiar roof like a flabby hat squashed down over the upper floor, as though it had been sat upon. Windows peered out from its folds like eyes. Pernille lived within sight of his bedroom window, the width of the street and a block away. He had never had reason to speak to her before today. A girl, older—why would he? Besides, she was weird. Everyone said so.

Now she would never speak to him again. He was appalled at himself.

He squeezed between parked cars, squares of blue paper taped to their windshields. That busybody from the café, Miss Grondal, forever leaving notes explaining who could not park where. He had received a dozen himself, for leaving his bicycle where she didn't like it, taped to the handlebars and smudged by rain. She noticed *everything*. It made him nervous. Especially now. He didn't want to be noticed. He had broken far too many laws. He crossed his road and passed the apartments and rounded into the courtyard behind. Were those kids still around? No. Thank goodness.

He was very late getting home and the courtyard was already folding into shadows. An enormous smokestack, once a part of the porcelain factory, rose from the overgrown middle and punctured a patch of rich, red sky above the rooftops. *Frederik's chimney*, he called it. Had done since he was tiny. A giant tapering column of brick, right outside his window. Apartments, six floors high, on two sides of the courtyard. Two long rows of tightly packed town houses to complete the square.

A steel staircase climbed to his own front door. Warm light in the kitchen window above. Home. Safe!

He let himself in. Listened for voices. Caught a familiar tuneless whistle outside. A screech and a crash. He opened the door a crack. His father, in his overcoat, scarf flapping, clambered to his feet, his bicycle on its side by the railings. "Ouch. Blast it." There was a good deal of dropping things, closely examined wheels, and then Father was at the top of the steps, his hand on Frederik's on the doorframe. "Open up, there's a fellow. What's the news today?" Without waiting for an answer, he was over the threshold, shoes flying, and up the stairs in his socks.

"The earthquake!" Frederik called after him, a bubble of hope popping up from inside. "The earthquake is the news. But it wasn't an earthquake, was it? Couldn't possibly have been."

He hurried upstairs to the kitchen, a disaster of cabinets around an old table, tall windows looking down on the street. The town houses were only wide enough for a single room per level. They stretched skyward, the living room above the kitchen, the office over the living room, bedrooms in the basement and the rafters.

Father had seated himself with the newspaper. He lost control of it, dropped a section, offered several colorful words.

"You're home very late today, Frederik," Mother said.

"Am I?" he said, sounding guilty even to himself. "Oh. Perhaps. Yes. I got, well, you know, delayed."

"Delayed?"

What explanation could he give? Any word of detention and he would be sent to his room, unheard, computer confiscated, allowance withheld. And that was before the summons arrived for his railway misdemeanor!

"How were your sandwiches?" Mother asked.

"What? Oh. A bit runny." He hadn't tried them. They'd been too mangled by all the falling over on the train. Could he mention the train? He was going to have to. He was suddenly nervous. How on earth was he going to start this conversation? "I'm not sure gazpacho goes in sandwiches terribly well."

"Nonsense. Not even with curried herring? We enjoy

all the lovely foods of this country. Like other families. We want to be like other families, don't we?"

And it hit a nerve. Annoyed him immensely. He *wasn't* foreign.

"We *are* like other families," he said. "Aren't we?"

"Of course we are. Other families eat herring and lovely, freshly made gazpacho."

But not so much together. Or in sandwiches. And who was he kidding? They weren't like other families. Never had been. Mother had long studied the local cuisine but without success. He always opened his lunch box out of sight of classmates, so they wouldn't taunt him with their correctly constructed salmon smørrebrød and their slices of Queen Charlotte cake, while he struggled to hold together whatever Mother had failed to master that day—venison with raspberries rather than red currant. Belly of goose with peach instead of plum. Errors that people from many places might entirely miss. But on Frederik's Hill, folk were particular about food. And where they shopped. And where one parked one's bicycle—and pretty much everything else. Mother's near misses betrayed him every day. As an outsider. A foreigner.

Father had disappeared behind his newspaper. A bold

headline stretched across the front: *Quake Never Happened, Says Mayor's Office!*

Frederik yelped. "Father. I have to tell you something."

"What, dear boy?"

"About the earthquake!" It *had* happened. If it hadn't, why was it news?

But Father folded the paper hastily, squashed it into a square. Headline hidden. "Hmm?"

"There *was* shaking in the night," Frederik said. "It woke me up!"

"Well," said Father, sliding the paper out of sight. "Vibrations, possibly. There were, possibly, some vibrations overnight. Some have said. Though many disagree. Best we don't talk about it. Mayor wouldn't like it. People might get the wrong idea."

"Which people?"

"Important people. You know, VIPs."

"The ones who are coming to the international festival?"

"Exactly."

"But the mayor doesn't realize what caused the shaking!"

"It was probably nothing. Best to forget about it."

"No!" he shouted.

There followed a silence. Father, flushed, peering over the top of his spectacles. Mother, in her librarian's cardigan, a hand on her hip and the other on a pineapple.

"What I mean is," Frederik said, "there's more to the story. I stumbled on something. I got on the wrong train. It wasn't my fault."

"Were you late for school?" Mother frowned.

"No," he said. "Well, a little, but that's not the point."

"What is the point exactly?" And now he was in the spotlight, had everyone's focus, and his mouth was dry, his hands moist.

"There was a tramp. A very smelly, dangerous tramp. He chased me, you see. Onto the wrong train. An underground train. It's completely secret. Passengers are banned. It runs right under our house. And the zoo. And the brewery. Oh, and the lighthouse!"

"Lighthouse?"

"That one!" He flung out a finger to point over Father's thinning hair and out beyond the window. Over rooftops of steep slate, a few streets away, to the clock tower on top of Municipal Hall. Hundreds of feet high. Except it wasn't a clock tower—he knew that now. Right at the top, fifty feet above the clock, was a curious structure he'd never thought to think about before. A cage of railings the height of three men, capped by a green copper dome. Huge panels of glass faced outward. And a light. A bright-white light that shone out over the whole of the Hill. A beacon. A lighthouse.

No one said a word.

He turned back to them. And they were paying no attention whatsoever. Mother was focused on dinner and Father on the paper.

"I'm serious," he said.

"Yes, dear," said Mother, without so much as a glance.

"There's a plot! A conspiracy. The tramp and the train conductor. They caused the earthquake! The underground railway is extremely unstable. It almost derailed. Shook like a roller coaster for over a mile. They're trying to blame the mayor! To frame her!"

Father chuckled quietly into the sports pages. "The things you get into your head."

"But it's true!"

"There isn't any railway, my dear, young chap. Underground? Where did you get that idea?"

"How do you know there isn't?"

"Well, I've lived here more than eleven years. I think I'd have noticed, don't you?"

"But what else could have caused all that shaking?" Frederik snapped. "It woke us up!"

"Don't take that tone with your father," said Mother. Her library cardigan was spattered with juice and her glasses were wonky from chopping. "You're already in trouble, coming home this late from school!"

He hesitated, lost his thread. The story didn't even sound believable to him.

"It is a lighthouse," he muttered.

"What was that?" said Father.

"Nothing. Nothing at all."

He watched Mother attack the seared remains of a duck. His appetite was gone. There was an unpleasant, fluttery feeling in his chest. It was like his world had suddenly changed shape. Nothing was what it seemed. And he couldn't get through to anyone. Not even his own family. What could he do? What could he say? What if he said the wrong thing? He might put them at risk. The principal's threats had been horribly clear.

He excused himself and headed for the stairs, to spend

some time with his telescope. But then he remembered—his telescope was all over the hardwood floor in pieces. Because of that train. It had shaken their house like a tambourine. It passed directly beneath!

Was it safe to live here?

He began to feel cold.

These buildings were old, 150 years or more. Were the foundations sound? Could they withstand another quake if that train derailed again?

He found himself turning and heading down to the basement. His parents' bedroom. Buried half-underground, like so many on the Hill, windows peeking out on the shoes of passersby. He checked the walls. No visible cracks. He stamped on the floor to see if it felt firm. Peered under the bed. Wasn't sure why. Peeked in the closet.

Stopped breathing. For a long, long moment.

On occasion, he had poked about in his parents' room, looking for birthday gifts before they were technically due. He had snooped in the closet. But what he was looking at hadn't meant anything to him until today.

At the back, behind the boxes and bags and shoes and old clothes, the wall was made of metal.

Old, rusting, curved metal bulged into the closet. The side of an enormous pipe passed through their basement and out the other side. And it reminded him immediately of the pipes he had glimpsed from the train. In the *Cisterns*. Could this old pipe beneath his house be somehow connected to those, more than a mile away, across the park? Did they join up? What were they for? And when that decrepit diesel went thundering by, might these pipes transmit the vibrations? Amplifying the tremors and shaking the house?

He tried to compose himself. He was overwrought. He needed a nap. He needed a think. He closed the closet. Headed upstairs. Paused at the front door.

Grabbed his coat on impulse. Called up the stairs. "Back in a bit!" And he nipped out the door before they had the chance to object.

The night was blue black. Traffic rumbled on nearby streets. Frederik stared at the ground where his parents' bedroom met the sidewalk. Where did that pipe go? Which direction?

That way. Northwest.

Toward the giant chimney in the courtyard.

The chimney had to be more than one hundred feet tall—a pillar of old bricks towering high above the roofs.

Very old bricks.

Old, damaged, and no longer maintained by anyone. Like the train.

So what might happen if that train caused another tremor?

He traced an arc in his mind from the top of the chimney to his house. If that thing toppled, it would hit his bedroom and slice down through his home like a knife through a cake.

"Oh no," he breathed. "Oh no."

CHAPTER 11

Breath and Bodies

He picked his way between the bushes to the overgrown heart of the square. The smokestack seemed to swell and grow until it was all he could see, soaring high into the sky. The brickwork was black and dirty. The mortar was old and flaking away. At the base of the chimney, attached to one side, was a hut, also of brick, perhaps at one time a kiln or a storeroom. What if the chimney had been weakened by the shaking from that train? He doubted anyone else had checked. If all this came down on top of his house, it would crush his family to mush!

He peered inside the hut. Absolute dark. A smell of damp. No point going in there till daylight. Wouldn't see a thing.

And then there was laughter bursting from the bushes. Voices and footsteps. Someone was coming. Lots of someones. The nasty neighbors. He slid inside the hut and hid in the shadows, holding his breath, chest on fire.

Silhouettes filled the doorway. Whispering. And then a light. A single lamp. Long shadows reached across the room.

"Hello?" He couldn't make out their faces in the dark.

The whispering stopped. A long, tense silence.

"Who's that?" A voice from the shadows, gruff and aggressive. Frederik Dahl Dalby. A tyrant from the nearby apartments.

His mouth was dry and he wanted to leave, but he couldn't get past them. He edged farther inside the hut, a dark cube of cold. The shadowy faces stared, none of them welcoming.

Lars Jacobsen stepped into a splash of light, waving the lamp his way. "Frederik Sandwich?"

"Yes."

"Who sent you here?"

Others waded into the stripes of lamplight and murk: Frederik Thomasen, Frederik Dahl Dalby, Calamity Claus, Erica Engel, Erik the Awkward.

"No one sent me. What do you mean?"

"The teachers. They sent him. To spy on us. He sits at the front of the class. He studies!"

"No!" he said. "Listen. There's something your parents should know. About the earthquake. We're all in danger!"

Nobody spoke. Nobody so much as blinked, alert staring eyes in the half-light.

"The tremors," he said. "The shaking? You know? In the night?"

"It's time you left," said Erica Engel in a tone as chilly as the principal's. "We don't associate with people like you."

"Hear me out," he said. "I've seen things. Secret things! You won't believe where I was this morning."

The heavy warmth of breath and bodies crowded in around him.

"There's an underground railway!" he told them.

Silence. Claustrophobic quiet.

"Directly beneath our feet!"

A cough but nothing more.

"A massive, old-fashioned diesel. It makes the most tremendous noise. *That* was what woke us all up in the night. An enormous, old train shaking the houses off their foundations!"

One of the silhouettes broke from the pack—Calamity Claus. He peered and sneered in Frederik's face. "A train?"

"Yes. Don't you see?"

"You're telling us it wasn't an earthquake but, in fact, a *train*?"

"Exactly," said Frederik. "It had to be. This is a very seismically stable region." He let it hang there. Gave them a moment to grasp the logic.

Calamity Claus sucked his teeth and scratched at the cast on his arm. "You," he announced, "are a very sneaky, little gibbernakker."

"No," said Frederik. "No, I'm not."

"The school says there was no earthquake." Frederik Dahl Dalby, a dangerous edge to his voice. "Therefore, there was no earthquake. The topic is closed, and anyone who raises it knows what to expect. Am I right?"

Heads nodded behind him.

"And yet here's a boy who is not from around here openly talking about it."

"Why?" Lars Jacobsen asked, approaching in a way Frederik really didn't like. "So he can collect names? Report back?"

"To get us in trouble," whispered Erica Engel. "*Again.*"

"But the shaking," Frederik blurted. "You felt it, didn't you? In the night? It woke me up. My telescope was smashed."

"We don't know what you mean," Erica Engel told him. "We didn't feel any shaking, and we haven't mentioned it since."

Frederik backed away, afraid and flustered. In the corner he noticed a shadow, darker than the others. A hole. The floor giving onto stairs. Steps leading below.

He pointed. "Then what's down there?"

Lars and Claus and Erica looked. The others kept their eyes fixed firmly on him.

"Oh, well, an enormous underground train, I expect," said Erica.

Cruel laughter bubbled and broke all around him. They closed in, jostling, sealing off his escape.

He edged the only way he could, toward the top of the stairs. The steps were old and in poor repair. He squinted down into darkness. He knew better than to go down there. A slippery surface, abandoned machinery—it was dangerous.

But so were these kids.

"Follow me if you don't believe me. I'll show you!" He didn't feel anywhere near as brave as he was trying to sound. He felt for the first step, took a chance, plunged into blackness, feeling ahead with outstretched hands. Down and down till he felt the floor even out in front of him.

He couldn't see a thing. Footsteps above and behind him. They were following. He had hoped they wouldn't dare. There was a flood of lamplight. Frederik Dahl Dalby and Erica Engel, breathing down his neck. He was in a rectangular room, damp and deserted, stains on the walls and bats squeezed into a crack in the corner, eyeing him, creepy as anything.

"Well?" said Frederik Dahl Dalby darkly.

"Well," replied Frederik, panicky now. "Let's see."

But there was nothing down there to see except damp and bats and broken masonry. A single doorway, completely bricked up. It must have led deeper inside the old porcelain factory at one time, but now it was only an outline.

He put a hand out to steady himself. Connected with something cold.

Metal.

Curved metal. Bulging out from the wall. Rusting iron.

Another pipe. No! The *same* pipe! The pipe from his parents' room, passing beneath the chimney and forming the whole side wall of this claustrophobic cellar. Heading right through and away beyond. He gave it a tentative kick with his toe. It rang, dull, heavy.

"Sewer," said Frederik Dahl Dalby.

"No," Frederik said. "I don't think so. It isn't buried deep enough. It must be part of the factory workings. A steam pipe perhaps, or water." And then it came to him. Could that be why it matched the pipes in the Cisterns? Had this once been the factory's water supply?

"You're lying to us, Flipper-rack," said Erica Engel, nasty and near. "There is no train and you are a liar."

Lamplight shifted around him. Breath on the back of his neck. He was suddenly scared. Didn't like this at all. He was surrounded in the dark, beneath a chimney that might fall at any moment. He twisted away and was suddenly running, not thinking, making for the steps. Climbing, stumbling. He picked his way through sneering children. Took a shove to the shoulder and a kick to the shin.

"Underground train? What an idiot."

"Then explain the lighthouse!" he blurted out, turning back to face them from the doorway. "The lighthouse on top of Municipal Hall!"

Howls and cackles, holding of bellies.

"Get out of our hut," said Erica Engel. "You don't belong."

He didn't wait another instant, ran for the bushes and over the cobbles and up the steps to the door of his house. Humiliated all over again. High above the rooftops, the band of red at the top of the brick chimney seemed to sway toward him. But it was only the motion of the clouds, a trick of the light. Nothing was shaking. Nothing was toppling. Nothing crashing to the ground except his self-esteem.

He opened the door and stepped inside the warmth.

There wasn't a soul in the world he could talk to. Not a soul.

He could still hear their laughter from here.

CHAPTER 12

A Dam Burst

He woke in the dead of night again. But not to shaking. He woke this time to darkness, silence, and a stomach cramped with worry. He slipped from the warmth of the quilt to the shock of cold boards under unready feet. He pried the blinds apart and peered at the chimney. There it was. Terribly big and terribly close. But upright for now.

He glanced over rooftops, toward the lighthouse that simply couldn't be. And it wasn't. Somebody had turned it off. No light, no glow. Just a fancy metal structure atop a brick clock tower, everything normal.

He had spent a whole day grasping for anything that seemed like normal. And now normal was back. But Frederik was not at all convinced. He looked hard. For anything unusual. He found it so quickly it stole his breath.

A blink.

A little flash.

And then another.

Not from the lighthouse, but across to the left, down near the corner of the street, a single flashing light at a black window set into a sat-upon roof.

Pernille's house!

What on earth was she doing?

Was it her?

Or was it someone else—an intruder, a burglar? The tramp, signaling to the conductor? He scanned the street for silhouettes, for anyone lurking. Nobody there among the darkened cars and empty doorways. The flashing was extremely persistent. Flash, flash, flash. Persistent and somewhat annoying. Right. So it had to be Pernille, in fact. Who could she be signaling to in the dead of night?

No.

Surely not?

The girl was *deranged*! What did she want from him now? In the middle of the *night*!

He closed the slats and sat on the bed and ignored the signals completely. He held out resolutely, wouldn't be swayed. She was insane.

But what if she was in trouble? Needed his help? She had saved his life. He owed her, didn't he?

He looked again and the flashing had stopped. Why had the flashing stopped? Had she been snatched? Overpowered?

He pulled yesterday's clothing on over his pajamas and picked his way down through the house by all the floorboards that didn't creak. He peered down the cellar stairs, listened for snores. He slipped his shoes on in silence and stole out onto the street.

The night was snap cold. In the darkness, the chimney was a thousand times his height. He made sure it wasn't moving. He hoped the pajamas beneath his trousers didn't show at the ankles. A girl like Pernille would notice that kind of thing and might never let it go. It was jolly cold and extremely late—or perhaps extremely early. He couldn't see the clock tower from here.

What was he doing?

Had he gone mad?

Why had he ventured outside in the dark? His parents would be furious. He'd be grounded for a month. He started back before he'd even been caught.

But the chimney filled the square of gloom above the courtyard like a massive exclamation mark, and his day replayed in reverse in his head: The chimney and the train and the tramp and the earthquake. His misdemeanor, his detention, his unkind words.

Something sinister was going on. A whole lot of sinister somethings, and if another was happening, he couldn't ignore it.

So he turned again and slipped among cars. He kept to the shadows. He found a deep, dark doorway across from the sat-upon roof.

He watched very closely.

No blinking light. No face at the window. Nobody there. Nothing.

Was she all right? Was she alive?

He waited. Where was she? Had he imagined it?

Feeling a bit of an idiot, he was just about to turn back

toward home again when the night was sliced and his heart was stopped by a terrifying hiss.

Ooh and it scared him. Oh boy, did it give him the willies. Though only for an instant, of course. He knew right away it was her, and it made him hopping angry.

"What are you *doing*?" he whisper-shouted to the shadows. "Go back to bed, why don't you?"

Pernille Yasemin Jensen, a tall silhouette in the shade of the alley behind the upholstery shop, swung her little pocket penlight and shone it right in his eyes.

"My little lemon," she said. "I simply knew you'd come."

Frederik, furious—though frankly he didn't know why—spent a fruitless minute spluttering at her disrespect for other people's bedtimes and insisting his name was *Sandwich*, thank you, and nothing else, edible or otherwise.

Pernille nodded and blinked in the streetlamp glow and made little clicks with her tongue. "Yes, yes, little apricot. Now breathe deeply and remember I owe you your life. I would do anything you need, and it seems to me that what you need is a friendly ear." She patted him and said very softly, "Tell me everything."

Now, perhaps you have heard the notion of a dam

bursting. You have probably never seen a dam burst for real, and Frederik hadn't either. He had never seen much of a dam, in fact, in that flat, wet country close to the sea, but something in Pernille's friendly gesture burst a dam in Frederik, and before he had time to sound alarms or organize sandbags, every detail of his day was gushing through the crack in his concrete reserve.

"The chimney is going to fall on my house. It'll squish my parents to pulp! That train! The pipes! The tramp! The conductor! Why will nobody listen?" he said at roughly three hundred words per minute. "I'm really, really sorry for what I said in the shop. I didn't mean it! It wasn't my fault. They'll send me to prison!"

Pernille rested her head to one side and stroked Frederik's hair. He let her do it—it felt such a relief—and then he remembered himself and flinched and swiped at her hand.

"You are forgiven," she said, "but only if you help me. We have a real-life, bona fide mystery on our hands, and I need your assistance. If *only* we were orphans. It takes an orphan to solve a mystery, you see. Nobody else will do. Are you certain your parents *are* your parents?"

Frederik panted and ranted some more and flapped his arms in the air until Pernille took a firm hold of one of them.

"In that case," she said, "there is only one recourse remaining to us. We must go to the mayor herself. No further delay!"

"What?" And off he went again, babbling, till she tugged his arm so hard it made an unhealthy cracking sound.

"Calm down. Let's take this matter to Her Ladyship immediately."

"Now?" he said, deeply unnerved by the risk that entailed—and also by the way his elbow had gone all floppy and loose.

"Now."

She sucked her lip in the amber glow and looked up and down the street, still grasping Frederik's hand. He realized suddenly what other boys might make of that, were they to glance from their windows.

"Come on," she announced, and before he had time to free his fingers, she marched off around the corner, dragging him in her wake past the front of her father's upholstery workshop and past the small pub and the yellow house and the blue house and the pond, straight for the imposing bulk of Municipal Hall and its sky-high, darkened lighthouse.

"What are you doing?" Frederik yelped, forced to trot to keep up. "Let me go! Where are we going?"

"To the mayor!" Pernille declared, ignoring a *Don't Walk* sign entirely and hauling him into the roadway. "We must tell her about that hobo hiding under her feet. The train conductor and the plot they are hatching. Everything. Her Ladyship will know what to do. She and I have a special connection. We shall tell her all, and Her Ladyship, the pillar upon which this community rests, our esteemed leader and inspiration, shall...well, she shall...well..." And there, she tailed off, rather spoiling the finale.

"But," said Frederik, pulled at high speed by an arm he feared was so stretched it may never again match the other and would protrude embarrassingly from the ends of sleeves, "it's the middle of the night. Municipal Hall will be closed. The mayor will be tucked up in bed."

"Not at all," said Pernille. "I know the mayor's ways. I follow her. She is my role model. She works tirelessly and without cease for the good of Frederik's Hill, and if you imagine she's going to take a night off with an earthquake on her hands, you are severely underestimating her."

"You *follow* the mayor?" he asked, rather stupidly.

"I follow her example," said Pernille. "Her path. In order to model my own. Her Ladyship rests but rarely. She gazes, they say, hour after hour, upon the whole of Frederik's Hill from a high turret atop the Municipal Hall, ever watching out for our welfare. For yours. For mine."

"A turret?"

"Oh, I rather imagine so. Don't you?"

"We *cannot* intrude on Her Ladyship in the middle of…" said Frederik, forgetting the end of the sentence entirely. For looming high in the dark at the top of the very tall clock tower—or turret perhaps to the fanciful—an enormous light had begun to glow.

"Her Ladyship stirs," said Pernille in a creepy kind of whisper. "The moment has come, little clementine, to introduce ourselves to my mama."

CHAPTER 13

Breaking and Entering

Your mama?" He pronounced it as she did—*m-mah*, to rhyme with hurrah. "You mean to tell me the Mayor of Frederik's Hill is your *mother*?"

"Yes," said Pernille. Her white hair wandered about them in the breeze. The glow at the top of the lighthouse was getting rapidly brighter and brighter. "I have every reason to suspect so."

"You suspect she's your mother, but you're not *sure*?"

"My adoptive papa, though I love him dearly, has not been entirely direct on the topic. Doesn't wish me to be hurt."

"You said your mother was Tahitian."

"My biological father is Tahitian. Or Ottoman. Possibly Persian. And so my startling hair must hail from my mother. It stands to reason. A native of frostier latitudes. A local."

"But you don't like the locals. You think they are prejudiced. And they think you're weird."

"Mostly that is true. Thankfully, my mama, the mayor, is of broader mind. Her international festival is proof of that. She is opening Frederik's Hill to the outside world. A grand celebration of our otherness. We will be embraced at last— you, me, and all the other weirdos."

"And what makes you so sure she's your mother?"

Pernille chuckled into the breeze. "Simple deduction, my little croissant. As everyone knows, one's missing parents are typically to be found close at hand, in positions of influence and power. Ergo. De facto."

"Where did you get *that* idea?"

"From books. Don't you read?"

"Of course I read. Schoolbooks. Astronomy. Science."

"No children's adventure literature?"

"Not really."

"How tragic. No wonder you're at sea in mystery scenarios. I shall have to lead. Follow me."

Frederik stumbled after her, the enormous Municipal Hall of Frederik's Hill looming ahead of them in the night. As accustomed as he was to seeing it, to checking the time by its clock with a glance from his bedroom, he found himself seeing it as though for the very first time, now that his companion was contemplating breaking in and presenting herself to the highest authority in the dead of night with a dubious excuse.

It was a vast red box—six windows high and twenty from corner to corner. It jutted out of the night, a sheer cliff of windows, every window as big as two men, and a broad brace of brick between each and the next. A sloping, red-tiled roof, yet more windows set into the slant.

Frederik had passed this building a thousand mornings and many more. He had seen it every day of his life. His father worked inside this building, had worked here for years, and yet never once had it occurred to him just how many windows peered out from those walls, how many departments there must be. He did some rapid mental arithmetic. Six floors by twenty by twenty again—more than two thousand offices. No wonder they needed a railway station! How would Pernille *find* the mayor among all those offices, even supposing she got inside?

She was marching, ramrod straight, hands behind her back. She was staring up at the lighthouse. This was ridiculous. She would never get in. The doors would be locked.

He was out of breath. He rested his hand on a chest-high wall—a stout brick wall with slabs on the top, at the end of the hedge, close to the long, flat front of the building.

He glanced over the wall.

There was a flight of concrete steps. Wide enough for ten men shoulder to shoulder. The steps disappeared into the ground. Into darkness. Underneath Municipal Hall. They were blocked at the top by a white iron gate.

"Look down there," he said.

She didn't. She pulled a strand of hair from her eyes and continued staring ever up.

A cold wind wound among them. Pernille's hair danced about her ears, her face dark against the dull night sky.

"Do you think this was once the entrance to the underground station?" he wondered.

"A question for Her Ladyship," she said. "We will quiz her about everything—the stations, the lighthouse, all of it. And we will alert her to the deadly threat to her borough. That frightful tramp and that poisonous ticket collector mean mischief, mark my words. We need the mayor's executive insight. It is very hard to get an appointment with my mama. Believe me, I've tried. But I'm hopeful that, at this time of night, her calendar won't be too cluttered."

She swiveled on one heel and grabbed Frederik by the sleeve. "Tell me, how are you at breaking and entering?"

"What?"

"Burglary. Forcible entry. Do you suppose she has an alarm?"

"We can't break in!"

"Of course we can. We're here on community business. Where's your sense of civic duty?" She flounced to the top of the concrete steps, and he followed her in a panic. They stood together, staring down the steps into a black void. The way was barred by the white metal gates. Frederik was relieved about that. Nothing was going to tempt him down there.

"We should come back in daylight," he said.

"Poppycock. The brightness of our wits will guide us." She bent forward, cupped her hands one over the other, and said, "Over you go, gooseberry."

He blinked back in disbelief. "I'm not going over

there," he said, and he pushed both of his feet very firmly to the floor.

"It's only a hop."

"I can't climb over the gates," he said, one of those embarrassing wobbles in his voice. "It's against the rules. It's trespassing."

"Those rules again. You do have such an attachment. Rules are for fools."

"What? No, they are not. Rules are the bedrock of this borough. They exist for all our sakes. Set down by the mayor herself!"

"Exactly. So I am exempt, you see. Family discount. Now lift up that leg and let's skip to it."

Now, maybe it was his sense of civic duty that led Frederik to hoist up his foot and let her boost him over, or maybe it was the worry that he would look a ninny if he was out-braved by a weird girl. But whichever it was, he found himself well and truly on the other side of the gates and the rules and any way back from the brink of the staircase plunging into the bowels beneath.

Pernille rested her hands on the top of the gate. "Down you go," she said. "Call out if anything attacks you."

"You're not coming?" His voice was suddenly very small.

"Of course not. Someone has to keep an eye out for the police."

"*Police?*"

"Naturally."

He tried to breathe. "I can't go down there alone."

"Take it slowly. Step by step. Let your eyes adjust. And remember, if the earth begins to tremble and pieces of masonry are raining about you, try to cover your head."

Frederik ventured a first hesitant step. Down the concrete stairs, between the brick walls, into the yawning shadow underneath Municipal Hall. He couldn't see. He needed a flashlight. Oh! Pernille had one!

But before he could ask, Pernille apparently decided step by step was not the approach after all. She leaned over the gate and gave him a gentle, encouraging shove.

In his surprise, he lost his footing. He tumble-skipped down stair after stair, his hands flailing out at the wall, but there was no rail and, in not much more than an instant of panic and swirling glimpses of sky, he collided rather heavily with a stone floor, on his side, at the foot of the steps, mercifully not all that deep but extremely dark all the same.

"Help," he said, though quietly, because he didn't want anyone to hear, least of all that madwoman. His whisper echoed. There was no light save that from the patch of gloomy sky at the top of the stairs. Alone in blackness, Frederik sprawled, winded and wounded. His heartbeat thumped in his ears, a little earthquake all his own.

"Did you trip?" Pernille's faraway voice bounced around the walls. "What can you see down there?"

He could see nothing, that's what he could see. He stretched his eyes wide, peered into nothing. *Let your eyes adjust*, she had said, shortly before shoving him down a flight of stairs. He vowed never to speak or listen to her again. Nevertheless, sure enough, as he gazed into all that nothing, his vision began to resolve. From the purple black, the vaguest outlines emerged. Very slowly, barely more than illusion. A dark tunnel, and a short way along it, two huge doorways leading under the building, twice, maybe three times the height of a man and as wide as they were tall. Each barred by a massive metal door, fat rivets standing proud on the surface.

Gingerly, checking for injuries but finding none he could really make Pernille feel guilty about, he got to his feet. He stepped forward slowly, feeling for the floor. He put an arm straight out in front and waited for contact with anything. Another step and another, and then the palm of his outstretched hand pressed firm against cold iron.

He pushed.

There was no give. He traced his fingers from side to side, found the rivets but no latch. The metal door towered above him, lost in blackness.

He listened. Very closely.

There was something.

Soft. Regular. A tap.

Another.

Footsteps. Coming closer. He couldn't tell which direction they were coming from. *Tap, tap*—footstep, footstep—closer, louder, and still he could see nothing but blackness and feel nothing but cold, and he shrank back, away from the door. A lunatic tramp lived down here, a tramp who'd threatened to gut him and sell his organs to goodness knew who or what! *Tap, tap, tap* and without any warning an ice-cold hand clamped across the side of his face.

"Aaaagh!" he hollered, lurching forward and banging his head against the door. "Aaaagh! Get away from me!" He waited, horrified, for whatever nightmare was about to be visited. He could hear breathing in the pitch darkness. And then he was blinded by an explosion of pocket penlight.

"My little dented date," Pernille announced from the glare. "Is something down here?"

"Yes!" he choked, even though it was dawning on him the something was her.

"Should we leave, do you think?"

"Yes!" he yelped.

And then her face lit up in front of him, clear as day. Only orange. The whole tunnel with it.

And then it went totally dark.

Then bright and orange. And dark again. And there was a wail. An awful howl. A terrible clatter assaulting their ears. An insistent and deafening ringing row, and flashing lights—orange, dark, orange, dark.

The burglar alarm.

CHAPTER 14

Nowhere to H!de

Never had Frederik run so fast. Gasping, legs burning, Pernille hauling him bodily over the gate at the top of the stairs and into the night. Leaving the mournful wail and the flashing lights far behind. Keeping to shadows, watching windows for any flicker of a blind. At one point he tripped, fell, and found himself on the concrete, facing back the way they had come. An office light was on. High in the corner of Municipal Hall, under the clock tower, looking their way. And was there a face? It was hard to tell. A woman perhaps? He didn't wait around to find out.

He spent the rest of the night, what was left of it, hiding

under the covers. Not sleeping. Not for a second. Panicked and paranoid in sweaty pajamas.

Saturday dawned bright and devilish cold. He was up before anyone else. Watching the street. No police cars. Watching Municipal Hall in the distance. No more flashing. No alarms he could hear from here. But were there cameras? Was he on video? How would they come when they came? Would they screech around the corner, sirens blaring? Or silently, stealthily, out of nowhere, hammering on the door? When? What were they waiting for?

Honey sunlight smacked the side of the clock tower. He could see slivers of sky through the tall glass lenses at the top. Blue, cold sky with thin, white lines of cloud. A walkway ringed those highest reaches. Shoulder-high railings, nobody up there. It wasn't a clock tower at all. How had he ever thought it was? That was a lighthouse. Hidden in full view of everyone, a twenty-minute train ride from the sea. But *why*?

"Frederik?"

He jumped and banged his head against the window. Turned to his mother, mouth open, nothing he could possibly say. Couldn't have looked more guilty, and she knew right away.

"What are you up to?"

"Nothing."

"It's something." She stepped to the window, looked the length of the street. "What is it?"

"It's nothing. I promise."

She looked at him, long and unblinking.

Father swept sideways into the kitchen in slippers and robe. Tossed the newspaper onto the table.

Frederik leaped at it, almost ripped it.

"Steady on," said Father. "I'm still reading that."

Front page. Bold headline. *Interest Rates on the Rise*. No mention of Municipal Hall. No alarms. No alerts. Nothing. Pages two and three, the same.

"What are you looking for?" asked Father.

"Nothing," he said too quickly. "Nothing specific. Not at all. Not to speak of."

"You're behaving strangely," said Mother, compiling a plate of ill-matched produce. "Watercress juice? A pickle pastry?"

Father's phone began buzzing, vibrating. Hopping sideways across the table. Father reached for it, startled. "Hello?"

A pause.

"You want me to come into work today? A Saturday?"

Nodding. Lips tight.

"I see. Right away? I see." He set it down, frowning. "The office," he said. "I have to go in."

"To Municipal Hall?" said Mother, annoyed. "On a Saturday?"

"There was a break-in," Father said. "During the night. The mayor saw the interlopers escaping. *Outerlopers*, she called them. One tall and one short."

Frederik's mouth was abruptly desert dry. He gripped the table so hard it hurt.

"Outerlopers?" said Mother. "On Frederik's Hill?"

"She's mobilizing all departments. Wants them found and brought to justice."

"But isn't that a job for the police? Or security? You're in rules and regulations."

"We're to draft some new ones," Father replied. "Stricter ones. There's a big crackdown."

"I think I'll go for a walk," Frederik said. He suddenly couldn't feel his legs. His voice had gone all croaky. He fell out of his chair, banged the table, backed toward the kitchen door.

"Oh no you won't," said Mother. "Not with criminals wandering loose!"

But Frederik wasn't listening. He was down the stairs and out the door, pulling his jacket about him as he ran. He stopped at the corner. Checked the street. Ducked low and used cars as cover. Crossed the road at speed. Banged on Pernille's front door and didn't stop.

Nothing happened.

He waited. Turned his collar up, dipped his head. Kept his face away from the traffic. Knocked again. What was keeping her? Nothing happening inside the upholsterer's workshop. No one there. Furniture stacked on benches, awaiting repair. Tools and fabrics. Brushes and bobbins.

"Come on, come on," he muttered, knocking again.

And then he caught movement. But not inside. Reflected in the window. Someone behind him, across the road. Outside the Café Grondal. He turned without thinking. And Gretchen Grondal stared right back at him without so much as a flinch, her notebook in one hand, a pen in the other. Watching his every movement like a python watching its prey.

Don't panic, he told himself. *I'm just a boy, calling for a friend.*

But then it struck him. His friend was tall. And he was short. They fit the description—the description was of them! And the moment a busybody like Gretchen Grondal saw the two of them together, the game would be up. The phone would be reached for. The police would be screaming down the street. And then what hope would they have? With his foreign name and her foreign looks. Who would protect them? Not the mayor. He didn't believe for one minute she was Pernille's mother or cousin or aunt or any other relation. That was a fantasy. A dream. They would be done for.

He dropped his hand. Put it deep in his pocket. He hurried away, making sure he didn't look back. Where could he go? Where could he hide? Him, a boy who behaved himself scrupulously, suddenly a suspect in a break-in, a misdemeanor, a double detention, and who knew what else? His poor, innocent family at risk. And meanwhile, the real criminals, that tramp, that train conductor, self-confessed enemies of the borough, were under Municipal Hall itself, planning mayhem.

Municipal Hall loomed at the end of the street. He had to get out of sight. Where could he go? Not home. They had his name, his description too. How many Sandwiches were there on Frederik's Hill? Just him and his parents. They'd find him in minutes. Mother would be all alone at the house. Should he go back? Protect her? It seemed like the right thing to do. It seemed suicidal. And he was *innocent*. He had to clear his name! And Pernille's. No one else could show the authorities what was happening under their feet.

Past the Ramasubramanian Superstore, along the side street, past the fire station, into the square. Where to now? The station? The mall? No and no. Much too public. Hundreds of people. Nowhere to hide.

To his left was the library, Mother's workplace. A place he knew well.

Quiet.

Discreet.

No one talked to anyone there. No one met your eye. They were all too intent on their books.

And there were thousands of books. Hundreds of thousands. Dating back generations. Documents. Records! There had to be records of a railway underneath Frederik's Hill, and where else would they be than the Frederik's Hill Central Public Library? If he could prove the railway existed, that would be *huge*. He would have a defense. He could raise the alarm! And then it would only be a matter of time till they stopped that train and found the tramp. The plot would be unearthed. Frederik would be cleared of all guilt. And no chimney would come crashing down on his parents' heads.

He sprinted to the library like his life depended on it.

CHAPTER 15

Frederik's Hill Central Public Library

Frederik crossed the center of a cube of space and light. The lobby of the Frederik's Hill Central Public Library. The chief librarian, Mother's supervisor, behind a desk. Bespectacled, mousy, fearsome. Readers waited with books to return and questions to ask. Everything was done by number—tickets were torn from a roll of numbers; turns were waited; numbers were called without a trace of a welcome or smile. A serious place, a hushed place. Conversations were held in whispers and still frowned upon. This was better. This was a place he could hide.

In the dead center of the atrium, steps led down and under the ground.

Viewed from the outside, the library was two floors high. But many of the books, the weightier ones, were down in the basement. Trips underground had not gone well in the previous day or two. It made him nervous.

Don't panic, he told himself. *Stay calm. Keep things in perspective.* The mayor had seen someone, outerlopers. Fine. But she didn't know who. Not yet. How could she? He could hide here in the library and look for the evidence he needed. He could turn this around. He knew it. All he had to do was avoid being recognized.

Oh no!

The librarians—Mother's colleagues. The library wasn't safe at all. Her workmates would do what they always did—draw attention, ruffle his hair, exclaim how *tall* he was becoming. Since he was becoming nowhere near tall enough, this was annoying at the best of times. Today it was a dire risk.

But underground, among rows of books, was better than anywhere else he could think of right now. So he took the stairs, winding downward. Voices murmured. Shoes squeaked on shiny floors. Tables and chairs among the shelves. Adults buried deep in battered books. A coffee machine dispensed plastic cups of thick, black smell. People moved slowly among the racks, heads tilted to read the spines of old hardbacks and tatty paperbacks, thick, thin, thousands of volumes.

The floor sloped away and swung to the right. He turned the corner and the way led right again. Right and down, right and down. The library was drilled into the bedrock like a corkscrew. Level after level of books, and the deeper he descended, the fewer people there were.

He stopped and checked behind him. Had the unnerving feeling he was being watched.

Only one man in sight—thin face in a fat volume, back turned.

He hurried on, thoroughly uneasy. The deeper he went, the dustier, the mustier it was. The books down here were thicker and heavier, as though the denser the topic, the farther they sank. Bound in brown leather and lettered in faded gold. Books with names he didn't understand. White walls gave way to darker decor—wood panels, peeling paint. Knowledge no one remembered to remember. Exactly the place to look for forgotten records.

Dark dead ends led away from the hallway. Occasional grown-ups, solitary, huddled in winter coats, faces turned from the world.

There were signs on the end of the shelves. *Anthropology. Arthropods.* He burrowed down from *B* to *D*. No one around. Was he safe? Yes. For now.

A sudden urge took hold of him and wouldn't be shaken. He turned down the next of the narrow rows, crowded on either side by books. *Earache, Earthenware.* A little farther.

Earthquakes.

An entire shelf.

Empty.

Not a single book or pamphlet or leaflet.

He stood and stared. Every shelf in sight was crammed tight with books and more books, except this one. It had been swept completely bare. He could see where books had been dragged through the dust. Recently. In numbers. In a hurry.

"May I help you?"

He nearly leaped out of his coat. Turned on one heel, ready to run, nowhere to run to, the way back barred. A slender woman, very severe. A librarian.

"I was looking for books," he stammered, guilty.

"Then the library," the woman said in a thin, threatening whisper, "is the perfect place to look." She smiled. Kind of. It was thoroughly chilling.

"There aren't any," he said. "Books. On this shelf here."

The woman's eyes narrowed to slits. "Removed. For cleaning."

"Cleaning? I see. Well, that explains it." But it explained nothing whatsoever.

"Wait," said the woman, peering closer. "I recognize you, do I not?"

"No," he panicked. "It wasn't me!"

"Young Master *Sandwich*? Madeleine's boy? How very *tall* you've become." She reached out a hand to ruffle his hair.

"Yes. Well, no. Well, thank you for saying so." He pushed quickly past her and made for the corridor, ducked downhill again. Checked back to see if she followed. She did not.

Where had all those books gone? Why was the earthquake being covered up? It had to be official. An order from on high. Keep it quiet. Don't mention the shaking. Don't disrupt the preparations for the international festival. But the authorities were playing into the plotters' hands! The criminals in charge of that train could trigger another earth-quake *any*time they wanted. There would be no warning. No way to protect the festival, the borough, or Frederik's family—unless Frederik himself could intervene.

A whirlwind was building behind him and bowling him along, deeper and deeper underground in semidarkness and stale air.

To a door.

Frederik's Hill said the sign. *Local History*.

And now he wasn't hiding.

He was hunting.

The door creaked. An older room by far. Bare brick and oak panels. He closed the door behind him, listened for footsteps. Nothing. Safe inside.

And then he wasn't. He could see through the floor! And the ceiling too! Instead of solid wood or tile, they were hazily transparent. Slabs of dusty glass held firm by iron frames. He could make out bookshelves towering two floors above. Beneath his feet, dug down into darkness, many, many more. Books in every direction, side to side, above and below, three dimensions of buried information. Over his head and to his left, he caught a movement. A face. A man. Staring down toward him, just for a moment. Then he melted into shadows. Police? He ducked behind a shelf. Not police. Mustn't panic. Much too scruffy. A ruddy face, dark with stubble. A bit like that tramp.

The *tramp*?

But no. What would he be doing in a library? He'd never get past the front desk.

Frederik had gotten cold all over. Little hairs bristled on the back of his neck. That feeling of being watched. He shook it off. Pulled himself together. He squeezed along a narrow row between the weight of paper and words. He watched his footing, unwilling to trust the see-through floor.

He looked up and left and right and down. Nobody there anymore. And here he was. Amid *Local History*. Masses and masses of it. If there was an explanation somewhere for the railway and the lighthouse and everything else that couldn't be, it would be somewhere in this room. But where? Finding it might take forever. The shelves were labeled, but not with names. Each bore a number, 2068.3, then 2070.1, and on and up in irrational, incomprehensible jumps. He sighed in frustration, and as his sigh died away in the hush, he heard a creak.

A single complaining floorboard.

He snapped around, but all he saw were half-darkness and cliffs of books disappearing into more of the same.

He held his breath.

Had he imagined it? He had imagined it. He listened hard. He was a long way down. The door of the local history section was closed between him and help.

He edged farther into shadow.

He traced his finger across the spines of old hardbacks. No kind of order that he could make out. Records of royal visits. Instructions for the control of pigeons. Rules and regulations for nursery schools. Rules and regulations for all manner of things—the loading of trucks, the shoeing of horses, the height and width of trees. Noise limits, age limits. All stamped with the crest of Frederik's Hill Municipal Hall and filed down here for public perusal, where no one would ever look. Deep underground. Hidden away. Just like the railway.

But records must have existed for a *railway*, surely? He worked along one row after another. He found plans for the hospital. He found wartime air-raid warnings, peacetime firework controls. Details of every facility built on Frederik's

Hill for two centuries. But no railways, no forgotten stations. He moved slowly, paid attention, and then with no warning at all, the floor creaked again and, straightaway, a *thump*. A heavy object dropped on the floor, a shocking *thwack* in the stillness. Frederik yelped, heart thumping like a drum.

Nobody there.

He waited, utterly frightened.

Police? The tramp?

They had found him. They'd hunted him down. He was going to be arrested. Or worse!

And out of nothing, from the shelf beside him, a whole collection of maps exploded into the air and twisted and fluttered to the glass floor, and before he could throw up or yell or run, a head squeezed out from the bookshelf itself, a great splash of white hair flopping down to the ground and a most unwelcome grin.

"Huckleberry!" she announced. "You realize, I suppose, that you're skulking in entirely the wrong row?"

CHAPTER 16

Vïola

What," he sputtered, "in heaven's name"—the shock was rippling through him in waves— "are you doing down *here*?"

"Skulking," she said. "Like you."

"I'm not *skulking*!"

He clutched at his stomach, held on to a shelf. She had scared the giblets out of him.

Her head disappeared, and he was left among an enormous pile of maps. He bent to pick them up. They shouldn't leave any sign they had been here. He found himself face-to-face with a pair of sneakers and blue woolen stockings.

"Decidedly," she said from somewhere above, "the wrong row, my pinto bean. Would you care to accompany me one row over? I have something to show you."

"*Why* are *you* down *here*?" he demanded.

"No idea," she said. "I was following you. But since I am here and I have discovered something you have not, are you really going to waste the day all creased and knotted up like that? Or would you like to take a little peek at what I found?"

Following him? How had she followed him without him noticing? He had been *so* careful. And if she had managed it, had anyone else?

With something of a flourish, she pulled a book from her waistband. A hardback. Old. *A History of Frederik's Hill*, the cover said.

"Listen to this. 'In 1902,'" she read, "'Mayor Mattias Mikkelsen ordered the construction of a grand lighthouse. It would shine from the roof of Municipal Hall into King Frederik's Garden Park and illuminate the fountains half a mile away.'"

Frederik's mouth fell open.

"'It further served,'" she went on, "'to light up the

zoological gardens, enabling them to open through the dark winter evenings.'"

He gasped. "It really *is* a lighthouse. But why did they turn it off?"

"It doesn't say. The fountains of Frederik the Tenth have been out of action for generations. That much I know. Her Ladyship promised to restore them, but there's no official word on when. Maybe for this year's festival. Now, come with me."

She led him around the end of the rack and into another bewilderment of books, far, far down in a green, forty-watt gloom. The air was still and thick with the smell of old paper. The shelves closed in. All he could see were Pernille's back and the tumble of her hair in the narrow canyon of shelves. It was most claustrophobic.

"There's something you must know," he told her. "The mayor's office has launched a manhunt. They're looking for us!"

"For us?" She stopped dead, and he collided with her back. "The mayor? Mama is looking for me?" *Mama* to rhyme with *hurrah*. *Pernille* to rhyme with *vanilla*. And people picked on *his* pronunciation!

"She wants us *arrested*!" he said. "For breaking in to Municipal Hall. We were seen!"

Pernille chewed on her lip for a moment. "That's inconvenient."

"We can't go home," he told her. "It isn't safe. Gretchen Grondal is watching your door. She nearly caught me!"

"That nosy witch."

"We need evidence, proof the railway exists. Then we can take it to the mayor, or her staff, and tell them what we know. But we must have the proof. No one believes the railway is there and until they do, we are toast."

Pernille patted his head and made comforting noises till he flapped her hand away. "Follow me," she said.

The corridor ended in an alcove. There were high racks on all sides, a table, and a chair.

"Viola!" she announced in triumph.

She had the wrong word, surely. Viola? "Do you mean the musical instrument?"

"Exactly," she said. "The instrument traditionally played, if one is French, at the moment of a great discovery. So. Viola!"

He didn't believe she'd gotten that right, but she

sounded so confident he didn't dare say, just in case. He edged alongside, close but not too close. She may have led him to her viola, but she was still a lunatic.

He squinted at the nearest shelf. *Civic Ordinances 1947, Volumes XXI to XXX.*

"What?" he said. "All I can see is books."

"This!"

In front of Pernille was an old, polished wood cabinet as tall as her and taller. In its face were hundreds of little drawer fronts, each with a label in a metal frame, each with a handle like an upside-down cup. Row upon row of little drawers.

"It's an index." She chose a handle and pulled. The drawer rolled silently and easily out from the cabinet farther and farther, a yard or more, till it sagged with the weight of its contents. She ran her finger over those contents and they fluttered. Frederik stood on tiptoe and looked over the lip. The drawer was full from front to back with little cards. Thousands of them, all the same size, sitting snug in the groove, some of them dog-eared, others crisp and untouched. Pernille pulled one out. *Hedgerows*, it said. *Height of, Regulations, 1912 to 1914. 823.3.*

"Alphabetical order," she said. "Shall we start?"

He threw himself at those drawers in a frenzy. *R* for *railways*. Hundreds of cards. He flipped through till his fingers ached, found nothing helpful at all. *T* for *trains*— the same again. Pernille collected a wad, flicked through them, lips pursed, wouldn't be distracted. What else could he try? How about all those abandoned stations? Was there a record of those? He went to *E* for *elephant house*.

Right away, he knew he was onto something. There were far more references to elephants than he expected. *Elephants, Viewing of. Elephants, Feeding of. Elephants, Diseases of.* And they dated a long way back—1910 and 1870 and the reign of King Frederik IX—and finally, approaching the end of the drawer, he found his own viola.

The card was green. The ink also. Faded, rarely touched it seemed, since it was noted and filed away in the depths.

Elephants, it said. *Underground Railway Disaster.*

All aflutter, he lurched away to find whatever the number referenced. Lower floors yawned beneath him, gloomy and still through the dusty glass. Pernille was left behind. An underground railway disaster on Frederik's

Hill! Involving elephants! This was *proof*. Had to be. The underground railway existed!

He found his way to a wall of great flat folders. Enormous leather-bound slabs, hanging side by side. The one he needed was heavy. He tugged it inch by inch and then in a sudden rush that bowled him backward across the aisle. He struggled along to the darkest recess, laid the folder on a table, turned on the lamp. He opened the flap. Newspapers! A pile of them. The highbrow daily his father liked, yellow with age and a little crispy. A month's worth, maybe more, beginning March 1, thirty years ago.

He studied the front page—a cluster of articles, nothing that caught the eye, just dry accounts of politicians decades out-of-date. He opened the newspaper, careful in case it crumbled or ripped, and took a look at pages two and three. Nothing again—trade disputes, television tittle-tattle—the same old, same old only older still. He leafed ahead to March 2, thirty years ago. Nothing in the headlines. So he tried March 3 and 4 and 5, grew impatient, and skipped a week, and it smacked him right between the eyes, leaped off the front page, and grabbed him by the windpipe.

Elephants Banned from Branch Line, it said. *Service Suspended Indefinitely for Repairs.*

Without so much as a moment's thought, he was off and running, down the dark hallway, hissing, "Pernille, Pernille! Come quick! I found it! Viola! Viola!"

As he rounded the corner at high speed, she walked right into him. Colored cards exploded into the air.

"Goodness, gooseberry," she protested. "Do keep your undershorts in order."

He grabbed her hand and hauled her to the reading table and stabbed his forefinger into the headline.

"March 13," he announced in triumph. "Thirty years ago."

Pernille patted her hair into place, or as close as it was likely to get, cleared her throat, and spent a long moment pretending to need a long moment.

"Look!" he insisted.

She leaned over the table. They both leaned.

In the wake of Thursday's railway disaster, the Frederik's Hill Municipal Underground Branch Line remains closed, a spokesperson for Municipal Hall announced yesterday.

"Transportation of pachyderms is henceforth prohibited," said

Kamilla Kristensen, Civic Secretary for Arts and Antiquities. "Such senseless loss of our precious heritage can never again be allowed."

"Kamilla Kristensen?" Pernille said. "But there must be some mistake. Kamilla Kristensen is not in arts and antiquities. Kamilla Kristensen is Her Ladyship the *Mayor*. Kamilla Kristensen is my mama!"

"But," said Frederik after a pause, "thirty years ago…"

"Of course! She was secretary for arts!"

"Look. A picture."

Tucked below the text, a black-and-white photograph of a startlingly attractive young woman, high of brow and a little stern and quite clearly the mayor herself some decades ago.

"Look at her hair," Pernille whispered.

"White."

"I *told* you."

But hair aside, he couldn't help feeling they didn't look remotely alike.

"What happened?" Pernille asked, terse. "Did you tear it?"

"Tear what?"

"The newspaper." She pointed at the paragraph below.

Outcry continued today at the catastrophic loss of and then there was a hole. Just a small one. So small he hadn't spotted it, with the print showing through from the page beneath. A hole one line of type high and half a sentence long.

Miss Kristensen insists, the paragraph continued, *that carrying elephants must end, given the appalling* and then another hole.

Frederik scanned farther down and found hole after hole, carefully cut, precise incisions that removed every detail of interest and made the article unintelligible. "So what happened? I can't tell what actually happened."

"As though," Pernille said in a low tone of conspiracy, "the article has been..." She paused and looked about, then whispered, *"Doctored."*

Frederik stared, confused. "Why on earth would someone do that? This is the front-page story. The national newspaper. Everybody in the land must have read it. This would have been common knowledge."

"But not anymore. Not thirty years later. I'm willing to bet everyone simply forgot."

"Until we discovered the underground branch line," Frederik murmured.

"Quite so, plum."

"It says the disaster was the previous Thursday. What date would that have been? The ninth?"

"March 9." She flipped back a few days. But March 9 made no mention at all. Dull economics, no disaster.

"Try the Friday after. Perhaps it happened too late in the day to make the Thursday edition."

Pernille turned the newspaper over and there was the next day.

Man Held for Attempted Murder, the headline yelled.

Police have arrested a local man for the attempted murder of Kamilla Kristensen, Civic Secretary for Arts and Antiquities.

"Attempted murder?" Pernille gasped in shock.

"There's more."

The man was later identified as… And another hole. A huge hole. The rest of the leading article torn out in its entirety. All that remained, rough edged and ripped, was a photograph. Two policemen making across Frederik's Square. Funny old-fashioned cars in the background and startled onlookers. Between the policemen, back turned and head bowed, a huge man was being led away. He had scruffy hair. Messy overalls with muddy patches. And there was something terribly familiar about the clothes, those stains. The man was slimmer and his face was hidden, but something in that posture, the bad-tempered defiance, was impossible to mistake. A ball of cold twisted in Frederik's belly.

"It's the tramp," he breathed. "Look at his hair. The muddy boots."

"The tramp tried to murder my mama?"

She turned to the Sunday edition and found another hole. She turned the pages one by one, and every mention of whatever happened thirty years before under Frederik's Hill, something involving trains and elephants, the evil tramp and Her Ladyship the Mayor, had been ripped away.

They turned to each other, mouths open.

"What can this mean?" Frederik asked. "And why would someone doctor this story? Who ripped away all the details?"

"There's only one person it could be," she said. "The one person with something to gain if this crime is forgotten."

"The tramp himself."

"Exactly."

"The tramp caused a rail disaster."

"In an attempt to kill the mayor." She grabbed

Frederik's arm. "And now he's back. And trying to cover his tracks by ripping his details out of this paper!"

Frederik's thoughts were spinning at breakneck speed. "*That's* why he's hiding under Municipal Hall! He means to try again."

"To finish her off," Pernille breathed. "Not just her festival but *her*. We must go to her right away! We must tell her."

"No!" he said. "We can't. Her people are hunting us!"

"But now we have proof! We can take this with us."

Directly below them something clattered, something hard falling on something hard. Both of them jumped. Eyes wide.

Frederik looked down.

Under his feet, blinking up at them through the glass floor, a face he recognized instantly. Bulging eyes and blotchy skin and yesterday's bristle.

"It's him," Frederik choked. "He's here! The tramp!"

They stared, paralyzed, through the murky floor at the tramp staring back at them. He raised a single fist and waved it violently above his head. He was yelling at them, but all they could hear was muffled and incoherent. Flecks of spit hit the hazy glass.

Frederik tried his best to come up with a measured course of action. He failed utterly. "Run!" he yelped.

And the two of them headed at reckless speed along the narrow aisle, glancing, terrified, down through the floor at the killer in the shadows.

CHAPTER 17

Guru

"Is he following?"

"Watch out!"

Crash.

Pernille ran into a poorly parked bicycle, toppled it over, fell across it, became entirely entangled, and spent precious seconds getting free of the wreckage.

"You're attracting attention!" Frederik worried, scanning the street for the tramp, pursuers, police.

"Why is he following us?"

"He isn't. He can't be. It doesn't make sense."

"He knows we *know*!" she said. "He saw us reading

those newspapers. The ones he doctored. He saw us getting on that train. He knows we know too much! He needs us silenced. Eliminated."

"Watch out, Pernille. Pernille, watch out!"

Bicycles tore through the intersection, fizzing by, scarves flying. A hundred homeward-bound Saturday shoppers with packed baskets. Pernille was engulfed in a cloud of fast-moving metal and legs. Bells clattered; voices were raised. "Get out the way! Look out! Watch your back!"

She pirouetted, arms flailing, white hair lashing like the sweeping arc of light about a lighthouse. She lunged for safety, curses ringing and pedals clanking and her coat all twisted and confused.

He hauled her clear of the onslaught to the safety of the sidewalk. Her grip was firm and cold and frightened.

"Look where you're going! You could have been hurt."

The traffic lights changed and the river of mayhem screeched and swerved to a halt.

"Come on," he told her. They made it across alive and raced along the narrow street. Homes and apartments hemmed them in on either side, six floors high.

She grabbed his arm. "Who's that?"

"Who's who?"

"Back there by the crossing. It's him! He's coming!"

The tramp was bludgeoning through the bicycle traffic, oblivious to the complaints.

"We must save ourselves!" she wailed. "Before we're cruelly silenced by that butcher."

They ran down the street, the busy flea market ahead—a crowd they could hide among. But just as they readied themselves to sprint across the street, Frederik realized: Municipal Hall! They would be visible from every window of Municipal Hall in broad daylight, and every department of Municipal Hall was on the lookout for them!

"Stop!" he yelped. They froze, exposed, at the door of the Ramasubramanian Superstore. Municipal Hall loomed like a vast cliff no more than fifty yards away. "We forgot the proof. We left the paper behind."

"You again," said Venkatamahesh Ramasubramanian, spilling out in front of them. "I have almost entirely undamaged confectionery for polite children," he told Pernille. "I have nothing whatsoever for ignorant boys like *him*."

Frederik twisted around in panic. The tramp was still

coming, marching doggedly. "Please," he said. "Let me apologize. I was unforgivably rude. I know that. Let me apologize in here!" And he grabbed Pernille, tugging her through the door and into the cool of the shabby little shop.

They threw themselves to the floor behind battered boxes and broken cookies. The floor was sticky. A refrigerator buzzed unhappily. So did the shopkeeper, glaring down at them, hands on hips.

Frederik peered between the shopkeeper's legs, toward the open door. A bus rolled by. A bicycle. Another. He barely dared breathe. Pernille folded her ungainly frame between his shoulder and the shelf. "Do you see the tramp?" she whispered.

"Yes!"

A massive, disheveled silhouette lumbered into view. The tramp was staring out across the street toward the hubbub of the Saturday flea market. Rubbing the palms of his hands on his filthy overalls. Frederik shrank back, just the top of his head protruding from the display.

"You are barred, young man," the shopkeeper said. "Please leave immediately. The girl can stay. Perhaps she might care for potato chips? Only lightly fractured."

"I can't go out there!" Frederik yelped. "I'm *sorry*. I really am."

The tramp had stopped dead outside the door, looking left and right, searching. For them.

"Call the police!" Pernille hissed at the shopkeeper.

"Police? I am extremely law abiding in all particulars."

"No!" said Frederik. "Don't call the police, whatever you do!"

"But we're in the clear! We have our evidence."

"We don't! We left it in the library."

"The mayor, then," Pernille said. "Call the mayor. We need to warn her!"

"Warn her about what?" The shopkeeper was panicking. Hopping from foot to foot in a way that was sure to attract the murderer's attention at any moment.

"About him!" She prodded a finger toward the street.

The shopkeeper turned to look. Stopped hopping. "Who?"

They peeped over the pepper and herbs.

Nobody there.

They waited. Nothing happened. The refrigerators rattled and buzzed. A pair of ants explored the syrupy floor.

"Where did he go?" Pernille whispered.

Very carefully, very slowly, Frederik crept toward the daylight. Bicycles hummed by. He poked his head outside. A huddle of people by the bus stop. Many more among the stalls of the flea market just across the street. But no tramp. He checked right and left and ducked back inside.

"Let's make a dash for Her Ladyship's office," Pernille said. "Even if he sees us, he won't dare to follow us there!"

"No! Not there!"

"But he's a *murderer*! Her Ladyship is in mortal danger."

"And Her Ladyship thinks *we* are the criminals, thanks to your midnight break-in. She won't listen to us."

"She will listen to *me*."

"For Pete's sake!" he burst out. "It's not safe. *Nowhere* is safe. This isn't some childish children's adventure story."

"Exactly right," she said. "At last you appreciate the seriousness. This is a real-life murder mystery, and only you and I can solve it." She paced the cramp of the corner store, her hair in her mouth once again. "Let's review what we know. The tramp attempted a heinous crime, underground, thirty years ago. Destruction, mayhem, and almost a death, somehow involving an elephant."

The shopkeeper leaned in toward Frederik. He smelled curiously of cumin. "Elephant? Did she say elephant?"

"Yes!" Pernille grabbed him by the shoulders. He looked terrified. "Can *you* tell us more? He was led away in shackles, we know that. He's very distinctive. A filthy, disheveled dropout with matted hair and staring eyes."

The shopkeeper nodded solemnly and made a clicking sound with his teeth. "Like a guru?"

"No," Frederik said. "No, no."

"My mother would have told you to follow him," the shopkeeper said.

"Follow *him*?" Frederik wailed. "He's following *us*!"

"He isn't a guru," Pernille said. "Far from it."

"A ragged man with staring eyes in the company of an elephant? Overnight earthquakes consistent with Ganesh himself? A guru, she would tell you. He will lead you to the truth, she would say. And this boy is in particular need of enlightenment."

"No," said Pernille. "He is a homicidal enemy of the mayor. He is her nemesis." Her mouth fell open in an almost inaudible gasp. "And that explains why she forswore her own daughter! She was forced to deny me, to protect me from harm!"

Frederik wasn't so sure about that, but a psychopath with onion breath was loose on Frederik's Hill. He had almost killed the mayor once. And now he was back. He had tried to erase all record of his crimes. He had gained access to the tunnels directly beneath Her Ladyship's offices—and to a locomotive capable of shaking the building apart. And *no one* other than Frederik and Pernille knew a thing about him. No one knew he was here.

It was very, very important, it suddenly struck Frederik, that someone else knew the tramp was here.

But where was he? Where had he gone? What was he up to now, and who would stop him?

No one.

No one at all.

"Mr. Ramasubramanian is right," he said. "We have to follow the tramp. We *have* to. We can't let him out of our sight until we find a way to raise the alarm."

Pernille fell uncharacteristically quiet, her shoulder against the shampoo. "That doesn't sound entirely safe."

"Safe? It's exactly the opposite. But what else can we do? We can't go to the police. They'll throw us in jail. And then what?"

"Then Her Ladyship would be defenseless. A sitting duck."

"Exactly. So we must find him. Follow him. Wherever he goes. Uncover his plans. Intervene if we have to. But we cannot let him roam the borough unobserved. Her Ladyship's life is at stake. My family's too." He stared up into Pernille's enormous eyes.

"He threatened to kill us," she said in a small, frightened voice. "Like some kind of fluffy animal. I can't recall which kind. It may have been guinea pigs."

"And Her Ladyship the Mayor is next." He stepped past the shopkeeper, opened the door, edged outside, scanning the street. No sign of the tramp. Which way had he gone?

"I really don't want to be dead," Pernille said.

"It's our duty," he told her. A little nugget of defiance was welling in his belly. "I was born on Frederik's Hill. I belong here. And I am going to do what's expected of me."

She seemed to hold her breath for a while, staring up at Municipal Hall. "If we save my mama, do you think she will thank us in person?"

"I know she will."

"All right then."

"A bag of bonbons for your journey?" came a mournful plea from behind. "Hardly ripped open at all."

But Frederik and Pernille were already heading away, into the street. To follow the homicidal tramp and save the life of Her Ladyship the Mayor.

CHAPTER 18

A Door In the Floor

They ran across the street, dodging a bus, a scooter, twenty lethal bicycles. No sign of the tramp in any direction. Bikes and baby carriages were propped and abandoned outside the weekend flea market. Municipal Hall rose above them like a dire warning. Windows and more windows. Eyes watching from any or all.

Pernille slowed at the top of the steps that led beneath the building. "Could he be down there?"

"No. He wouldn't get past the alarm. Keep moving. We mustn't be seen here."

They slid through a gap in the hedge into the camou-flage of the crowd. Tables piled high with old tools and pans and toys. People everywhere. Haggling. Arguing. Picking over bric-a-brac like it was treasure. Frederik and Pernille ducked under arms and nipped between legs, feet slipping on dropped hot dogs, making slow progress through the crush. Deaf to the rumble and snort of the buses, the bad music, the chatter. Where was the tramp? Frederik stood on tiptoe. Scanned faces, backs of heads, every row. The tramp was nowhere.

"Let's head toward the park," he said. "He must have gone that way."

Through the noise and out the edge of the flea market, past the pond, along the alley between the antique store and the flat, white side of the never-open gallery. The tall north gates of the Garden Park were directly ahead, among the trees, the crest of Frederik's Hill set into the arch.

"I don't like this," Pernille said. "We're terribly exposed."

"I don't like it either, but we have no choice."

They jogged through the gates and into the trees. It was already afternoon. Thin sunlight filtered over Frederik's Hill. Shadows were soft, buildings wore their bright colors a little less pronounced. Ripples crossed and recrossed the dark-green canal that wound through the Garden Park in crazy, mazy loops. Mothers and toddlers were gathered at the water's edge, feeding the ducks. The herons leered in their hundreds from their nesting trees. Watching.

Watching a man.

An enormous, disheveled man in dirty overalls.

"It's him!"

They ducked quickly behind a tree, tucked their arms in, held their breath.

"What is he doing?" she hissed.

They peered out slowly.

The tramp was marching toward the canal. He was waving his arms. Bystanders were paying him sudden attention. Full attention. Alarmed attention. The tramp was shouting. Loudly. Madly. "Get away! Get away! They are coming!"

"*Who* is coming?" Pernille fretted.

"Flee! Hide!" The tramp was ranging from side to side, harassing adults, startling ducks, terrifying children.

"He's going to hurt someone if they don't get out of his way," Pernille said.

And getting out of his way was clearly foremost in everyone's mind. Folk were scattering, not looking back, gripping their children and making tracks.

"Get away from here!" the tramp hollered after them. "*Run!*"

Everyone readily complied, shocked and afraid. In less than a minute, there was nobody left by the canal except the tramp.

Frederik and Pernille watched from the cover of the trees, fascinated and appalled.

The tramp came to an abrupt stop by the water. Standing on something, a slab of some sort, set in the ground. He hunched his shoulders, staring intently at his feet. He bent to a squat and examined whatever he was standing on. Then he twisted his head as though listening for something underground.

He stayed completely still.

Then he wheeled around, scanning the area, looking directly their way.

They pressed themselves flat to the back of their tree, holding their breath.

Branches moved in the breeze.

A squirrel scampered close, stopped, stared at them, twitchy.

No sound at all save for the lapping of the water and the chatter of the ducks. It was hard to say how long they waited. Seconds? Minutes? Time had slowed to a terrible crawl. Eventually, swallowing compulsively, Frederik took a look around the tree toward the canal.

No one there.

No tramp.

Gone. Again!

He stepped cautiously into the open, watching for any sudden movement, eyes on the bushes, checking the paths that wandered away through the park. *Where* had the tramp gone? Which direction? Along the canal? Around the edge? Through the middle toward the castle?

He made for the spot where the tramp had stood. Set into the cinder path, among the herons and ducks and all the varied doo-doos they had strewn, was the most unlikely thing.

"Look!"

"A door," said Pernille. "A door in the floor."

It was painted soupy green, like the canal. Slatted

wood. A heavy door with a hinge across it, at the side of the path, by the water's edge. An ancient iron padlock looped through a thick iron ring. It was a rather ordinary door, like the front door of a house. Except it lay completely flat in a pathway in a public park.

Frederik checked over his shoulder. No tramp. No one.

The doorway led directly into the ground.

"What could be under there?" Pernille wondered.

Frederik knelt and rattled the padlock. Hooked his fingers under the door. He tugged. It budged begrudgingly. He pulled harder. The door lurched. The padlock fell open on the path.

He froze. Now what?

He took a deep breath, straightened his back, and lifted the door. Peered beneath. Absolute darkness. Absolute cold. And very deep.

"What can you see?"

"Nothing at all."

"Did he go down *there*?" she said. She kept a wary distance from the black, rectangular hole.

"Surely not," he said. He scanned the pathways again. Lawns puddled with rain. Brush whispering in the breeze.

Geese squawked, never quite drowning the far-off rumble of traffic. But no tramp. No sign of him.

Chill wafted up from below the ground—but no light whatsoever, no sound. Frederik stared down past his toes into the void.

"You go," said Pernille. "I'll wait here for a bit."

"Are you out of your mind?"

"Someone has to follow him, pancake. You said so yourself."

"But it's *dark* down there! And we have no idea where it goes. He could be waiting. Knife at the ready."

"I have my pocket penlight. I will lend it to you if you promise to take care of it."

Unaware of the recent rumpus, new families were wandering their way—several adults and a number of children, throwing breadcrumbs for the ducks. No one looking directly at him, but in that way that suggested they sort of were. A toddler in a Viking hat toddled closer. A mallard pecked and fussed around.

"We can't go down there," he murmured. "We have no idea where it leads."

"Isn't it obvious?" she said. "It's a secret passage.

It leads underground, to the secret railway. And his secret lair! He's heading right now, as we speak, toward Municipal Hall. To carry out his evil plan. To murder my mama!" She gave an anguished little squeal and made for the doorway.

"Wait!" he said.

"We must stop him!"

He tried to get in her way. Missed his footing. Missed the lip. One foot plunged suddenly into the gap. He toppled. Grabbed at the edge. Bashed an elbow. Managed a kind of strangled yelp, and then it all went dark. He was flailing, falling, frightened silly. His hand hit something cold. He grabbed at it. Clung on for dear life. Found himself dangling in darkness from some kind of rung. A ladder set into the wall. Gasping freezing cold air. Hands burning. He waved his feet around in his terror, found another rung. He clung grimly to the wall. A circle of daylight high above his head, and Pernille's silhouette staring down.

"Are you alive, dear croissant? Please say you are!"

"Pernille," he managed. "Help!"

But by *help*, he meant help me *up*. Help me *out*. Grab hold of my hand. Stop me falling any farther. He didn't mean pull up your stockings, drop yourself over the edge, and plant a muddy shoe in my face.

"What are you *doing*?"

"Such drama," she muttered, her toes perched precariously on a metal bar just inches above his nose. He couldn't see what she was doing. There was a pause. A grunt. And the heavy door came swinging over and down. Darkness engulfed them. There was a bang as the door hit its frame, and then a long, appalling silence.

The sound of dripping far below.

And then a dazzling light blinded him completely. Burned his eyeballs. He lurched away in shock and banged his head against the hard, cold wall. The beam of Pernille's pocket penlight wandered about his head.

"Turn that off!"

"Be quiet, baguette. I'm trying to get my bearings."

By the narrow beam of a flashlight designed for little more than searching under a sofa, Frederik took his first look at his latest predicament. It was gunmetal gray in all directions. He twisted in panic.

Trapped! They were trapped! They were in a tube. A vertical, steel tube. Airless. Freezing cold.

"Go down," Pernille whispered. Her words echoed and hissed around his head.

"We're not allowed."

"Good grief! Is the tramp *allowed* to murder innocent officials of the borough? Go down!"

He felt for the next rung down and the next. The underside of the door in the floor was ten feet above him now. His hands were going numb. His head was spinning. He couldn't see. And then a splash. His feet were instantaneously wet. Wet and cold. There was a breeze across his ankles.

Pernille kept coming, pushing him aside, playing the flashlight erratically around him so he could hardly see what was what.

Another splash.

"Ugh," she said. "Oh, how ghastly."

The flashlight steadied, pointed at their feet. They were in a rather filthy puddle but on firmer ground at least. Their heads were still in the tube they had come down, but their legs and midriff were in another one, passing perpendicular across the base. A pipe. A big, fat, horizontal pipe. The height of Frederik's chest.

He recognized it instantly.

The curve of the iron, the rivets, the rust. The same pipe that ran through his house and the hut at the foot of the chimney.

Only now, he was trapped inside it.

CHAPTER 19

An Hour of Agony

Which way?" Pernille wondered.

Frederik's feet were half-immersed in murky water. It looked and smelled as though it had been there a very long time. He stepped higher up the sides of the pipe, where it was drier, legs splayed. He slipped. Splashed his ankles, saturated his socks. He grabbed hold of the rungs welded onto the wall, the rungs that climbed to the door in the floor and to safety. They couldn't stay down here. Better to get aboveground, go to the police, tell all, and hope to be believed.

But the door was a very long way up. Very solid. Very

heavy. Why had she closed it? How would they open it again? Heave it from underneath? How? They couldn't hold on to the ladder and push the door at the same time. They would fall.

"This way, I think." She began to edge along the tunnel without him.

"Wait!"

"We can't wait," she said. "Mama is in danger. We must hurry."

"This is insane! This is suicide!"

"Stay with me, pita pocket. I'm afraid to go alone."

He swallowed. Tried to be calm. "Not that way," he told her. "Come back. Municipal Hall is somewhere this way."

A hand either side to steady himself. A deep breath of unpleasant air. He ducked his head and maneuvered himself at a most uncomfortable crouch inside the metal pipe.

The pocket penlight searched ahead but showed them little. The pipe was long and straight and round and very dark. Water pooled in places. Where had the water come from? What if more came? What if water suddenly flushed along it and washed them away? They could drown!

Frederik struggled to a dry spot and rested, dizzy. Why

was he dizzy? Lack of oxygen? Poisonous fumes? Pernille panted and splashed along behind.

"Are we there yet?" she asked, and her voice seemed to stretch and twist and reach out along the pipe in an eerie moan.

He picked his way forward. Water splatted. The pipe rang with his footsteps. He kept going. Came to a fork. A tube leading left, another ahead. "Which way? Straight?"

"I don't know," she said.

"Straight is best. Don't you think? I think so." He tried to sound sure. Tried not to think about the murderer who might be waiting in the shadows ahead. They were down here to find him, but what if they found him? Panic bubbled up inside him. The pipe was curving more and more to the right. Wasn't that the wrong direction? Should they turn back? Was it getting wider? Another fork. Then a three-way junction. They took the broadest pipe each time. That was best. Frederik's back ached from bending, his legs from squatting. Another junction and a pipe as wide as a road. Stretching ahead into nothing. What if they never found a way out? No. Silly. They would be fine. Just keep on going. Municipal Hall was no more than half a mile from the door in the floor. How long could it take? Not much longer, surely. They might be somewhere under the flea market by now. Maybe? No? How much farther?

What was that?

The pipe itself seemed to yawn. A groan. Low and dreadful. Like a voice—an unearthly voice rising from darkness and damp and despair.

He yelped. He wanted to turn and run. But Pernille was right behind him. And where would they go? He couldn't remember which way they had come. They had taken too many turns. Too many random tangents. They were trapped in a nightmare! The groaning rolled and echoed, changing and folding and seeming to never end. Had it come from ahead or behind? What *was* it? The tramp? The murderer? Coming to rip out their entrails and leave them for the rats? He clapped his hands to his ears and whimpered. Tried to think of something scientific. It had to be something scientific. Stresses in the metal, that's what it must be. The expansion and contraction of the iron from changes in temperature, the pressure of the earth above. Logical. Rational. Nothing sinister. Nothing unnatural.

What did the tramp say was down here?

Zombies.

"Pernille," he whispered.

"I don't like this at all," she whimpered back.

"We have to get out."

"I agree."

"By any way we can find."

"I'm with you."

They half stumbled, half ran into the blackness, the pocket penlight helping hardly at all. He found one side of the pipe and ran his hands along the metal, feeling for changes, searching for any kind of exit. He couldn't stop swallowing. Pernille made odd little sobbing sounds like a puppy caught in a trap. They were caught in a trap! They would never get out! They would never be found. They would waste away. They would starve. They would freeze. They would fall and drown.

"Which way?" he groaned, and his voice bowled ahead of them.

"Shhh!" she hissed from behind.

"What is it?"

"Shhhhh!"

He stopped dead. It seemed to take an hour for the echoes and whispers to subside. An hour of agony.

And then he heard it.

A rumble. A steady, familiar rumble. Somewhere above their heads.

"Traffic!" he said.

The pocket penlight swept the ceiling of the pipe. Rusting iron. More of the same. The beam traced down the wall and…there! A dark hole.

They all but exploded into the space—another pipe— then a junction turning upward, narrow and slippery, rungs set into it, just like the one they had come down. Frederik climbed, hand over hand, reaching above to feel his way. It felt like he climbed forever. And then a sudden lack of air. Everything close. Everything tight. The top of the tube. A metal disk. A manhole cover! He planted his feet on the highest rung, braced his back against the steel, and pushed.

There was a groan. A stubborn resistance. A moment of despair. And then a *pop*. Light flooded the tube. Brilliant daylight. The rush of cars. Frederik heaved the manhole cover aside, scrambled up through the gap and onto flat, damp concrete. A sidewalk. Pernille clambered after, grabbing his leg and hauling herself out. The edge of the park, halfway along, where it met Frederik's Parkway and the open-air ice rink. A skater skidded to the edge of the rink and stared at them, confused. Buses and trucks rumbled by. Municipal Hall was no closer than when they first entered the pipe. They had missed it entirely. But that didn't matter. Not anymore. They were out! They were safe! They were still alive!

The skater swept away around the rink. Frederik gulped great lungfuls of fresh air. Pernille curled herself into a ball against his side and said nothing at all. And not far away, never one to miss a potential customer, Henrik Hotdog, infamous vendor of suspect food, leered at them from the window of his cart and called out, "Hot dogs? Anyone for hot dogs?"

CHAPTER 20

Henrik Hotdog

F rederik couldn't stop shivering. He wasn't sure if it was the cold or the horror, but something down in that pipe had crept into his bones and wouldn't let go.

"What was that noise?" Pernille whimpered. "That awful moaning."

"It was like a voice," he said. "Like a cry of pain."

"Or many voices. Merging into one long howl of agony."

"Like zombies. He said there were *zombies*."

"Could there have there been *other* murders? Grisly killings that no one dares speak of? Are the bodies hidden

down there? Is the tramp a serial killer? That must be it! We must tell someone. Before it's too late! An adult. *Any* adult!"

"Hot dogs, you two?" Henrik Hotdog beckoned to Frederik, smiled—sort of—tipped his head back, made a most disturbing noise, and spat into his frying pan. It made Frederik want to retch and heave and leave in a hurry. On the other hand, it shocked him out of his shivering. Henrik Hotdog was the most obese, objectionable slob on Frederik's Hill. All children hated the sight of him—the sight, the sound, and especially the smell. But then Henrik Hotdog hated children, so they were basically even.

Henrik Hotdog sold hot dogs from his metal hut on wheels, here at the edge of the ice rink, wrapped in a cuddle of custard-yellow buildings from the reign of Frederik the Third or so. Winter and summer, in rain or sunshine, hot dogs to the adults he disliked intensely, hot dogs to the children he detested. He was a miserable miser and nobody liked him and he didn't like them back.

However.

He was the only adult at hand.

Could Henrik Hotdog help in some way? No. Surely not? Surely they ought to find someone better? Someone they could turn to. Someone who was liked and trusted. Someone such as, well, such as, well…such as who exactly?

"What can I get you?" Henrik sneered. "Chili dog? Boiled pig? Clotted blood pudding for your girlfriend?" He pulled a piece of old paper from his pocket and used it to smear his phlegm around the pan.

"She's not my girlfriend," Frederik explained in a hurry.

"No kidding. Much too pretty for you." He granted Pernille a smile. She shuddered and backed away.

Henrik Hotdog was not, in fact, Henrik Hotdog's real name. Henrik Hotdog's real name was Henrik Hødtøg. Hødtøg, however, was unpronounceable. Even the natives of Frederik's Hill struggled with its silent consonants and glottal stops. And so Hotdog he had become, like his long-gone father before him. From his pitch by the park, he made a healthy living from very unhealthy food. How? The *name*. Henrik's father had started the business with the proceeds of shady shenanigans before retiring abruptly to the Costa Del Sol to live among suntanned gangsters and women of ill-advised wardrobes. But by luck, he had named the business after himself. And his name just happened to be Frederik. The inferior gristle the Hødtøgs peddled for higher-than-average prices was snapped up greedily and gobbled and belched by generations of rosy-cheeked skaters and cyclists and children with inadequate parental supervision purely because of the name above the hatch: *Frederik's*. The business had become a landmark. Directions were given by it, even though the cart itself was trundled back to its garage each night to return restocked the next day, once Henrik managed to flop out of bed.

"We need help," Frederik said. It sort of slipped out. He couldn't contain it. "Help us!"

"Help you? What are you talking about? Bloody kids. Are you buying something or what?"

Frederik glanced at the spit-smeared pan and crinkled his nose without thinking. "Oh. No, thank you."

"What's the matter? My hot dogs not good enough for you?"

"No. Well, that is, well, hot dogs are not good for anyone. Nutritionally speaking. You know."

"You don't know what you're talking about, you little drip. Hop it before I clock you."

"But we don't know where to turn," Frederik pleaded.

"This is a hot dog cart," Henrik Hotdog barked. "Not a counseling service. If you're buying hot dogs, get on with it. Otherwise, don't waste my time. I've got an appointment to get to anyway. An appointment with the mayor."

And without a millisecond's delay, Pernille was at Frederik's shoulder, shoving her face through the open hatch, in dangerous proximity to the owner. "The *mayor*? Did you say an appointment with the *mayor*?"

"What's it to you?"

"You're meeting the mayor? Where are you meeting her? When?"

"None of your business."

"Oh, but it *is* our business!" She seized his greasy apron and didn't flinch at all. "Where is she? Tell me!"

"All right, all right." He shrugged her off, took a step back, rearranged himself, as though that made a difference. "There's a meeting. About the enormous summer shindig. She's choosing the caterer. I need to be there."

"You?" said Pernille. "The International Midsummer Festival? I hardly think Her Ladyship will choose an unhygienic sausage cart to feed her foreign guests and dignitaries!"

"Bog off, you hoity-toity twerp. What's the matter with hot dogs? Do-gooder, are you? Bloody vegetarian?"

"Where is the meeting?" Pernille screeched, raising herself up on her tiptoes and glaring through the hatch.

"Here," he retorted and flung the scrap of greasy paper at Frederik. It hit him on the head, bounced off, and stuck to the ground in a most off-putting way. "Details on there, if you want them." Henrik cackled with laughter, frowned, farted, and yanked his shutters closed with a clatter.

"Pick it up!" Pernille shrieked.

"I'm not touching that!" Frederik said. "It's covered in fat and phlegm!"

"Oh, don't be so prim."

She peeled the paper off the pavement and teased it apart with her fingertips. It tore a little. The edges flopped over. But still visible through the grime and spit, a picture—a crowd of people, fountains, fireworks exploding above them against a sunset.

Her Ladyship the Mayor's International Midsummer Festival, it read. *The largest public gathering in the history of Frederik's Hill! Catering tenders to be finalized at the Frederik's Hill Zoological Society extraordinary general meeting.*

"When?" Pernille exclaimed.

"Tonight," Frederik read. "Seven o'clock."

"Where?"

He pointed. *Old Elephant House*, it said.

"The elephant house? We went there! On the train. The underground train. We saw it!"

Frederik gulped. Put his hand over his mouth without even knowing. There was a pounding in the veins behind his ears. Icy cold down the back of his neck. "And now we know," he whispered hoarsely, "why the tramp went down into the tunnels. Now we know exactly where he's headed."

"To the elephant house," Pernille breathed. "To murder Mama."

CHAPTER 21

Thinking Unilaterally

et's phone the police," Pernille said. "An anonymous tip-off. They'll never know it's us. Hand me your cell phone."

"I don't have one," he said.

"Whyever not?"

"Don't believe in them." He tried to hide his embarrassment. Wasn't about to tell the truth. Had no need of a phone because no one talked to him. "Use your own."

"I never carry it," she said. "I keep it in a decorative case in a box in a drawer in my bedroom closet. One shouldn't get too close to those things. They melt the brain cells."

"No, they don't."

"That's why they're called *cell* phones."

"No, it isn't. What are we going to do?" He stared at the manhole cover, still out of place, only partially hiding the deep, dark hole.

"I'm not going down there," said Pernille. "Never again. There's something very wrong in those pipes, bodies or zombies or something unspeakable."

"There's only one thing for it. Come on."

He marched at speed through the main park gates. The statue of King Frederik the something or other stared out, past the hot dog cart and along Frederik's Parkway to the city beyond, its corkscrew spires, the tallest rides of the carnival grounds, and the huge, white windmills out at sea.

The lawns ahead were awash with crocuses, white and purple painting the green.

"This is a much better idea," panted Pernille behind him. "We must think unilaterally."

"Don't you mean *laterally*?"

"Both."

They hurried along the wandering tracks among ladies with dogs and old men with sandwiches, ever south and west. Past the Japanese teahouse, the pagoda, across the canal, and across it again, to the foot of the steepest slopes of Frederik's Hill itself. Grassy ramparts climbing almost sheer to King Frederik's Castle, a broad slab of yellow stone with rows of white-framed windows and topped with the national flag. Across a canal bridge one more time and up the scree of gravel that looked on the Royal Zoological Gardens.

Railings. Water.

The foot of the zoo opened onto the Garden Park, giving passersby a free view across the dust of the lowest and largest enclosure. The animals were kept in not by a fence but by the depth of the pond. Strolling at leisure in the Garden Park, the folk of Frederik's Hill could look all they liked, across the water and the dust, and almost always there would be elephants. The greatest show on earth. Wandering the dry ground, showering themselves with clumps of dirt, picking at straw with the ends of their trunks.

Today, oddly, there were none. But there was no time to wonder why. Frederik lifted a finger and pointed up the hill. "*Viola!*" he said.

The Royal Zoological Gardens of Frederik's Hill had two elephant houses. To their right, the newer of the two was very new indeed—brand-new and state-of-the-art. Half-buried in the hillside. Terra-cotta stone partly covered with earth and grass. On the roof, staring straight up into hazy sky, were two glass domes, like enormous insect eyes. The new elephant house had been the talk of the town for years, from the grand design competition to the first foundations, the mayor's opening ceremony, the fanfare, the fireworks, and the pictures on the front page of every paper. It was big, bold, modern, and expensive.

But farther up the hill, a pyramid punctured the air. A high, red pyramid roof of nineteenth-century tile, little windows in its highest reaches and, holding it up, a row of stout stone pillars and a puzzle of orange brickwork. Bars on the windows, boarded-up doors. The old, original, disused elephant house of Frederik's Hill. The brickwork, the archways, the iron bars were unmistakable—and were *exactly* like the ones they had seen down in the darkness, from the window of the train. A disused elephant house with a disused station all its own, hidden away from a public too preoccupied with the brand-new replacement and its giant, wrinkled residents to notice.

"He'll sneak up from the railway tunnels," Pernille said.

"And no one knows to watch for him. Not the police. Not Her Ladyship. They're too busy watching for us!"

They rushed up the grassy ramparts, through the trees, out of breath. The afternoon had disappeared, between the corner shop and the door in the floor and the pipes and the hot dog man. Only forty minutes left till the zoo locked its doors for the night. Two hours more till the extraordinary general meeting and, if they weren't quick enough, an extraordinarily gory murder.

"We have to get to Her Ladyship herself," he said. "Face-to-face. And no one else can see us. We can't afford to get detained."

They ran among the linden trees, across the gravel, along the side of the castle, warm yellow with afternoon light. Beyond the high, spiked fence was the zoo. Strange whooping cries from creatures unseen, birds or apes or something else entirely.

"Let's think this through," he panted. "We can't go into the zoo. That psychopath might be in there already. Let's wait outside the gates, watch for Her Ladyship's car, and flag it down before she puts herself in harm's way."

But Pernille was like a runaway train. She swept out of

the park and onto the street. Groups of people were heading away from the zoo entrance—kids with balloons, adults scowling. Hundreds of bicycles, new and old, were leaning on railings, up on stands, wedged into every gap. There were baby carriages, strollers, skateboards. Frederik picked between tangled handlebars, was bumped and bumped again.

"Wrong way," a woman complained.

"Mind yourself, kid."

"Pernille! Wait!"

To his relief, she stopped a short way from the entrance, hanging back behind a pillar, out of sight of security.

"*Pomegranate*," she hissed. "Give me some cash." She gestured toward the turnstiles.

"Cash? Where's your annual zoo pass?"

"Haven't got one."

"What?"

On Frederik's Hill, *everyone* had an annual zoo pass. It was such good value. It paid for itself with only three visits and gave unlimited access for twelve full months.

"Never previously felt the need," she said. "And these prices! Extortion!"

"No problem," he told her. "We'll wait here. Much

safer. When her car arrives, we'll warn her and they can whisk her away to safety."

"No. She might be inside already. Give your zoo card to me! Once I'm inside, I'll toss it over the fence and you can follow."

Frederik almost laughed. If this wasn't a matter of life and death, it would have been funny. "Only I can use my card," he said. "It has my name on it, and my picture."

"I'll hide the picture with my thumb."

"No! We wait here. Watch for the mayor. Raise the alarm. That's what's expected of us. We're not breaking any more rules. There's too much at stake if we're caught."

She leaned in close, her nose to his. "The mayor of Frederik's Hill is in mortal peril from an enormous, violent anarchist who smells of *onions*. And you want to follow the *rules*? Do what's expected? *Someone* must save her." She stared at him with her enormous eyes and didn't blink for longer than he thought possible. "Who is going to save her if her own daughter won't?"

He raised his hands in exasperation. "So what's your suggestion? You think we should do the *opposite* of what's expected?"

"Ooh! Good idea."

"No! We can't even be sure that you *are* the mayor's daughter. It's just a theory. It's wishful thinking."

"I am *sure*." She narrowed her eyes and pursed her lips and scared him a bit.

"All right, listen. We could ask the woman in the ticket booth if the mayor is already here. How about that?"

"Certainly not! That woman might be in league with the tramp. Or the police. She might have pictures of us."

Yes. Actually that was true. And what if the mayor *was* here already? Wandering, oblivious, into a death trap?

"Stay here, then," he said. "Keep a lookout. Don't go anywhere. Don't do *anything* unexpected."

He slipped through the tangle of bodies and babies, his shortness an advantage for once.

"Cherry!" she called after him. "Wait!"

But his annual pass was in his hand and his head was down and the turnstile was turning, the gatekeeper nodding and stepping aside. "We close in thirty-five minutes, young man."

"Thank you," he mumbled, avoiding the gatekeeper's eye. He burst from the crush and into the open savannah.

There was a *Welcome* sign and a huge map, but he knew his way by heart. He began through the zoo at a jog. Extremely alert. Ready to turn tail at any threat. The kiddies' train deposited kiddies. Families struggled to the exit. Whiny children were towed toward home in rented handcarts. The crowd was ebbing away. It meant less cover. He had to be careful. Ultra-careful. He would head for the elephant house and take a peek. From a very safe distance. To see if the mayor was there. If she wasn't, he would back away. Wait outside. Safe and law abiding.

Camels chewed and watched him trot by. Lions prowled forward and back.

By a railing, balancing on one leg, heads swinging side to side, twenty tall flamingos with shocking-pink plumage.

At the end of the railing, balancing one legged, head swinging side to side, a tall girl with shocking-white hair.

"Pineapple!" she said. "Whatever kept you?"

CHAPTER 22

His Very Own Rule

He stopped in his tracks, dumbfounded.

"How?" he said. "How did you get in here in front of me? How did you get in at all? You haven't got a pass!"

"Details," she said, with a dismissive wave of the hand. "Let's get a move on. No time to lose."

"Did you enter the zoo without *paying*?" he asked her, appalled.

"The opposite of what they expected, my baguette. It's brilliant. You should patent it."

"You're out of control!"

"Oh my goodness. Look out behind you!" She flung up her hands in horror.

Frederik twisted and ducked, expecting to be set upon and suffocated, enveloped in the powerful arms of a stinking hobo with dirt on his clothes and appalling breath.

But no. There was nothing. The same flamingos, the same bored camels. He turned back to protest, and Pernille was gone, marching down the slope.

"See?" she shouted out. "Brilliant!"

He almost popped with outrage. He'd told her to stay outside. Entering the zoo without paying was punishable by fine and a lifetime ban. His own father worked in the Department of Rules and Regulations, and he had printed the signs for exactly this rule at home one evening. Frederik had helped! This was his very own rule! To see it flouted so blatantly stole his breath away. In eleven or thereabouts years on Frederik's Hill, he had never seen anything so brazen.

He stumbled after her, spluttering, checked the distant clock tower above the trees. The zoo was closing soon. They would have to get out before then or they'd be spotted, arrested, and reported again. Rules were rules! How else could a borough like Frederik's Hill maintain its standards?

Then again, the mayor was in dire risk of death and that wouldn't go down well at all. Not with a major public event only months away. They couldn't obey every little rule all the time. Not if it meant that tramp breaking the biggest law of all—the law of life and death! So he swallowed his sense of civic duty in the interests of civic duty. He broke into a run. When needs must, he reflected, a virtue doubled is a something or other. There was a saying. He couldn't remember the saying, but his mother had a saying and knowing there was a saying helped ease his conscience as he abandoned all his principles entirely.

"Wait for me! Pernille!"

The trail led away from the bears, skirted the wallabies, dipped through trees, and there, in front of him, hogging the hillside, the one-time centerpiece, now abandoned, of the Royal Zoological Gardens—the original, venerable, redbrick, hundred-and-something-year-old elephant house. Its pyramid roof reached almost to the clouds. Long and tall, turrets at each corner, topped with smaller pyramids. Wrapped by a scruffy enclosure. Bay doors and rusting equipment set along its flank.

He slowed, took shelter behind a shrub, and watched

for movement. But the only movement was Pernille, marching along the side of the building at high speed.

"Come back!" he hissed.

She waved a hand dismissively and carried on around the corner, out of sight.

He broke cover and chased her. To the back, the working side, removed from the public, storerooms, straw bales. Conveyor belts for delivery of fodder and removal of epic quantities of dung. Wheelbarrows sat stacked, broken, forgotten. Heavy padlocks on the doors. Boards covering the windows. No way in.

Pernille kept going, no attempt to be discreet. The tramp could be *anywhere*, and if he saw them, their chances were very thin indeed. They'd be gutted like Chihuahuas, their livers sold off as maracas. Where was he? Waiting? Lurking? Sharpening his knives?

At the front of the building, stone pillars as thick as trees supported a portico that looked out on the park and the lighthouse, high above rooftops. Steps led up and between the pillars to two green doors. Pernille breezed up the steps and between the columns and tried the door in broad daylight and clear sight of a party of the elderly.

Then she hurried back. She was agitated. "Locked tight. And there's a sign. It says the extraordinary general meeting is for the esteemed patrons and benefactors of the zoological society only. You're not one of those, I don't suppose? Not with your iffy name. We *must* get inside. We're going to have to get creative. I need you to think like an orphan. Can you do that? Tragic abandonment. Get the picture? Deep breath. What would an orphan do?" She closed her eyes, fists clenched, lips clamped tight.

"What are you talking about?"

"Think!" she commanded. "Think like an orphan."

"I don't know how an orphan thinks," he snapped. "Why would I think an orphan thinks differently than how I think? I don't think how I think because I'm *not* an orphan."

"Oh my long johns," Pernille chuckled. "Certainly you do."

An indistinct announcement crackled above the shrieks of birds and primates, something about six o'clock, something about personal belongings.

"We should leave," he said. "We're not supposed to be in here."

"There you are, you see. Nothing at all like an orphan."

And this time it really annoyed him. "What," he demanded, "do you imagine an *orphan* would do instead? Break into the elephant house through padlocked doors and accost the mayor, unannounced? Is that what an orphan would do?"

Pernille opened those enormous eyes as wide as they would go. "Genius! They'll never see it coming! I knew I was right to pick you."

"No! You're a maniac. I've had enough of this. I'm waiting somewhere safe for the mayor. If you want to do something different, *you* figure it out. You're the one with no mother! *You're* the orphan!" He set off with a stomp, made it two paces before she caught the back of his collar and almost strangled him.

"This way," she hissed. "Follow me! *Quick!*"

She darted the other direction, gripping his collar, and before he had time to croak, he tripped and banged his knee on the concrete.

"Come on, get up!" She tugged, and he was forced to follow, no time to think, looking wildly about for whoever they were fleeing, and when he saw no one pursuing at all, he kept running anyway, couldn't help it. Anything was better than being carved open by a vagrant who wanted to sell his kidneys. He ran and he ran, and the more he ran, the more he found himself unaccountably thrilled to be getting away with whatever it was he was getting away with, even though he had no intention of getting away with anything. A wicked giggle bubbled in his throat for reasons he couldn't even begin to explain.

"Where are we going?" he shouted out.

"The monkey house," she barked. "To the *monkey* house."

"Why?"

"Because you doubt me *still*, my croque monsieur. Because you will not be told. And you therefore must be shown!"

"Shown what?"

"The truth!"

"In the *monkey house*?"

"In the monkey house!"

CHAPTER 23

Nothing at All Like an Orphan

The monkey house was gloomy and muggy. The air was thick—and many degrees warmer than outside. The lights were off and only a halfhearted splash of day from a dirty skylight high above.

A glass wall looked into three small rooms, in each a tree and a pile of rocks. And monkeys. Baboons in the nearest, big puffs of fluff, eyes too close together, and livid-pink behinds. Next, some kind of macaque, small and golden, swinging wildly about the place on a vine. In the third, a black-and-white, long-armed something, hanging from a branch by its tail. All of them staring at Frederik as if to say *the zoo is closed, young man.*

"What now?" he panted.

"Now I prove how profoundly wrong you are," she replied. There was something alarming about her tone.

She walked to the glass, her back to him. She stood very still, facing the monkeys. "Chatter, chatter, chatter," she said.

"Pardon me?" said Frederik.

"Be quiet. Chatter, chatter, eek, eek, eek."

"What are you doing?"

"I'm not talking to you."

Frederik sprayed laughter and spit without meaning to.

"You don't understand," Pernille snapped.

"Nor do the monkeys."

She whirled on him, alarmingly tall in the gloom of the monkey house. "Don't you read books? Don't you know anything? The monkeys would understand me all too clearly if I *were* in fact an orphan. A detail firmly established in contemporary children's adventure literature. Orphans can talk to animals and animals understand. The monkeys clearly do not understand me, no matter whether I chatter or eek or ooh. Orphans can do all kinds of things. They can solve mysteries, pick pockets. Some of them can fly!"

Something stopped him chuckling. Something he only sensed.

"I cannot!" she said in a way that was entirely too intense. "I cannot fly. I cannot solve mysteries. I cannot talk to animals, and they cannot talk to me. I am not, repeat *not*, an orphan! Do you see? This proves it!"

A baboon watched her closely, picked its nose, and ate the rewards.

"I didn't mean to upset you."

"I *have* a mama."

"Of course."

"She is somewhere. She is!"

He felt like he was on the edge of a precipice. "Hasn't the upholsterer told you anything?"

Her shoulders sagged. He could see she was trying not to let them. "No. Only that it would be too painful to tell me. 'Let it lie,' he says."

"But you don't."

"I *can't*. But I can't find any proof either! I can't solve the mystery of why she abandoned me. Proving once again that I'm *not* an orphan. Proving she *must* be still alive. *Now* you understand," she said with icy calm, her eyes fixed on his, "why it's *so* important that I reach her, save her. Her Ladyship the Mayor simply *must* be my mama. She has no known children, she's about the right age, and she lives just down the street. Who else could it possibly be?"

She threw open the door and headed outside in a hurry.

"Wait! I'm sorry!"

The early evening was terribly bright after the dim monkey house, the air cold and fresh. Pernille was halfway down the steps, surveying the pathways. The zoo was closed. Nobody around.

"I've upset you," he said. "I didn't mean to. I wasn't thinking. I'm not very good with people. I haven't got many friends."

But the apology was split in two by the roar of a motor and the screech of metal on metal. Through the trees they saw a tractor dragging a trailer with big bags of feed. It made an unholy din.

"Run for it! Run!" Frederik wailed.

As quick as anything, Pernille dashed off. He bolted after her, the tractor a roar at their backs. They wove among shrubs, hugging shadows. Pernille zigzagged, breaking out into the open.

"*Wrong way!*" he hissed at her. "*Wrong way!*"

The tractor was closing in on them. Pernille was completely exposed. She faltered, out of ideas.

"This way," he shouted. "The old elephant house!" He leaped a wall and rushed into the long shadow of the building. She sprinted after him. The tractor choked and popped behind them, and he was too frightened to look back. Two doors set into the brickwork. Flat, windowless steel doors. He ran to the first. No handle. Couldn't budge it. Tried the second, grasped the knob, and twisted and shoved. The door complained, a terrible screech. He set his shoulder to it, glancing back across the dirt. The tractor was in clear sight. He gave an almighty push, and the door jolted open just enough to squeeze through and into deep darkness. Pernille followed with a grunt, coat snagging on a nail. She ripped it free and tumbled into the dark alongside him. They heaved the door shut, out of breath, out of courage, out of ideas. They braced all their weight against it and prepared to fight to keep it closed, to barricade themselves in.

Every second seemed like an hour. Frederik's heart drummed.

He tried to breathe. To think.

He could hear water dripping. The floor was cold stone. Patches of something soft. Straw, it might have been. It rustled. It smelled of something sour. Light spilled in a thin strip from the side of the door and died away in a blur. His eyes would not adjust. He couldn't tear them from that strip of light. It was surely a matter of seconds till there were footsteps outside and a massive shove and the door was thrown wide. Any moment. Any second now. Soon. Really, really soon. He waited. He continued to wait. Soon surely. Anytime now.

"Well," said Pernille in the darkness.

"Quiet," he spat. "Be quiet!"

"Righty-o," she said, as clearly as anything, like nothing extraordinary was going on at all.

And against all sense, sure enough, nothing extraordinary happened. No door burst open. No zookeeper appeared.

Frederik pressed his ear to the door, listening for the slightest sound.

But the sound that came was not what he expected. A sudden scrabbling from the far side of the room.

"What was that?"

"What was what?" Pernille replied from exactly where the noise had come.

"What are you *doing*?"

"Searching," she said, a disembodied voice in the dark.

"For what?"

"For a way out, of course. I can't see my own nose in here."

Frederik squinted down to see if he could see his own nose. He couldn't. He wasn't sure he could under any circumstances—not in focus anyway. It was too close and too down and too in-between, and while he was busy failing to find it, there was a click and a scrape and light spilled across the room toward him and painted his toes. Pernille had found her way out. Or rather, a way farther in—a sliding door leading deeper into the disused elephant house. Her silhouette stood momentarily still at the open end. Then she was gone.

What was she *thinking*? Anything could be waiting beyond that door. The tramp! Or wild animals. Snakes. Frederik was very uncertain about snakes. In fact, he was equally uncomfortable about alligators, bears, cheetahs, and right through the alphabet to zebras. Zoos were dangerous places to go poking around. No way was he going through there. He'd broken quite enough rules for one day. If Pernille insisted on risking her life, then let her. He would wait right here and see how long it took for her to scream.

It was a firm decision, and it felt good to be back in control of his own destiny.

Regrettably, at just that moment, somewhere beyond the sliding door, a terrified girl began to scream and scream and scream.

CHAPTER 24

One Long, Twisted Leg

Frederik Sandwich, alone in the dark, fought the urge to flee for his life. Ahead of him was an enormous sliding door that led to he didn't know what. To a silence broken only by echoes of Pernille's final scream. She had screamed three times at the top of her lungs. Not playful squeals, but screams of mortal fear. Screams consistent with confrontations with killers or wild, carnivorous creatures. He felt utterly cold. There was no more noise. Nothing at all. No stabbing sounds, no moans of pain, no howls, no growls, no crunching of bones between jaws. Should he flee or go forward? Risk

his life to rescue a girl who might already be dead? Or simply run away?

Where would he run away to? Home? Some lonely hiding place? Any one of the many places he wasn't welcome and didn't belong?

Just minutes ago he'd been laughing, running, almost enjoying their desperate mission. He couldn't remember the last time he'd felt like that. Had there ever been a time? And then he'd upset her. Been terribly harsh. She was only a kid, no matter how lanky and wordy and weird.

And she was his friend.

She actually was.

He didn't feel out of place with her. He didn't have to try to be someone he wasn't.

He crept forward a few paces. The straw rustled. He flinched. The sliding internal door was open just enough. He stuck his head through the gap.

Couldn't hear whimpering. Couldn't see blood.

He squeezed sideways into space. A large, white room with a shiny, tiled floor. Three times the height of any normal room. Hushed. Dim daylight filtering through square windows close to the ceiling, high above.

The room was full of chairs. Neatly arranged in rows.

On either side of the room there were big square cells behind iron bars. Tires lashed to the railings with old rope.

No tramp.

No tigers.

He checked very carefully.

No crocodiles. No snakes. Nobody and nothing but chairs.

At one end of the room were two wooden doors, and above each door a sign. *Entrance* said one; *Exit*, the other. The doors Pernille had tried and failed to open from outside. This was the public hall inside the old elephant house. All set up and ready for the mayor. In those huge cells beyond the bars, the elephants had once lived. Cramped. Claustrophobic. An elephant jail. A nineteenth-century prison of iron bars and great metal rings and bolts and locks.

There was no sign whatsoever of Pernille.

His footsteps slapped and echoed on the tiles. He tried to stop trembling and swallowing. Pernille might be dead, and if she was, he was sure to be next.

"Hello?" he said, but so softly he hardly heard it

himself. Had someone or something dragged her away? He checked every alcove and empty cell. Where could she have gone?

If only he had stayed with her, she might still be alive!

If only he had fled, turned tail, slipped out into the open air, and ran for the gates for all he was worth. He could have gone to the mayor, to his parents, even the police.

The place was deserted. Still.

And then he felt a shock wave in his shoes.

He stared at them.

No. It wasn't his shoes, but the floor. A wave seemed to pass through the floor, and everything started to rattle, the metal bars, the tires on chains, the rows and rows of chairs.

"Another earthquake," he breathed, barely able to believe it. "No. The train!"

Had the tramp dragged Pernille underground and onto that train? Was he whisking her away to some gory fate? The shaking seemed to swell, to build. Getting closer, not farther away. As if the train was arriving, not leaving. Metal clattered and wood creaked. He had to find Pernille fast, before she was smuggled on board! Which way could she have gone?

Steps led up to an iron grille. It spanned the width of

the hall, sealing off the last few yards. In the wall beyond, there was a huge sliding door leading out of the hall to darkness. The door was open a little. He gripped the bars and stared through them, a head width between each. The bars hummed and vibrated with every tremor. He tugged. Nothing. Immovable.

What now? There! Farther across the grate, the bars were hinged. A gate in the grate. He grabbed and heaved, and the gate swung open. Tipped him down the steps in a tumble. It made a devil of a noise. He looked around in panic. No one there. He picked himself up and ignored a sore elbow and limped through to the sliding door, a solid slab of steel. Open. Just a little. Just enough.

He squeezed through the gap.

A dark tunnel, high and arched, walls of crumbling brick. It smelled of dust and disuse. A gloomy passage, big enough for an elephant, leading into shadow. He took a step forward.

The trembling stopped.

Just like that.

He felt for the wall, steadied himself. Waited. Tried to breathe.

"Pernille?"

He peered ahead but couldn't see anything.

Stillness.

No more shaking.

Nothing.

"Hello?"

The floor dipped away, leading down and into the hillside. Was this the way to the underground station? Had to be! These bricks were the same. As were the arches and bars.

"Hello?" he called out, louder now, echoing down the tunnel.

But the reply did not come from the tunnel.

It came from behind and right by his ear, and it came with a sudden, violent odor of onions. "Hello."

Frederik was paralyzed, unable to think or cry out or run. A huge hand closed tightly on his shoulder. Hot breath played across the side of his face. Foul-smelling breath.

"The early bird," the voice said, "catches the worm, they say."

With a sudden jerk, he was turned around and now he was looking up at the man. A huge man. An ugly red-faced warty snort of an evil-smelling tramp.

"But I seem," said the tramp, "to have caught my worm unusually late in the day."

Frederik closed his eyes and tried to prepare himself for the violent removal of his innards. But instead, he was propelled at speed in the direction he had come from. The tramp marched Frederik out of the tunnel, through the bars, and across the public room with all the chairs, filthy fingers gripping his shoulder far too tightly for him to escape, pushing him forward at such a speed he could barely keep from falling. He couldn't breathe. He couldn't speak or squeak or even think. He was going to *die*. Pernille was dead, and he was going to die.

"How did you get in?" the tramp demanded. "Tell me or I'll feed you to the seals."

"Door," Frederik whimpered, pointing vaguely across the whitewashed hall.

"Which door?" He brought his bad breath far too close for Frederik's digestion.

"Over there, the sliding door."

"The fodder room? How did you get in the fodder room?"

"Broke in," Frederik said, far too terrified to lie.

The tramp marched him to the open door, examined it closely. Frederik could smell fresh air. He gathered himself, ready to twist and run. But the tramp gave a tug, and the door slid shut with a crash that rang around the rafters. From a deep pocket in stained pants, the tramp produced a padlock. He closed it through the hasp. The moment was lost. His chance was gone. He was locked inside the old elephant house with a murdering madman.

"Move," the tramp demanded, pushing roughly. He steered Frederik with more force than necessary around the last row of chairs, past the locked entrance and exit doors, behind a pillar. There was a door with peeling paint and insets of cloudy glass. The tramp slipped a key in the lock. Behind the door, a spiral staircase twisted upward. "Up there!"

Frederik stumbled step by step, up and around, till he didn't know which direction was which or how high he had climbed. Just as he thought he might fall over with fear and dizziness, the staircase opened onto a cramped space. Crazy tapering ceilings sloped high overhead and inward to a point. The pyramid! He was inside the pyramid roof of the elephant house. Utterly alone. Utterly frightened. There were no windows. The space was divided in two by a wall of old boards. Under the eaves at the far side, an unmade mattress with grubby sheets, a battered chest of drawers. Dirty, dung-encrusted clothing littered the floor. Muddy boots. A single rickety chair.

The tramp gave Frederik a shove from behind, forced him past the wooden partition into a kind of kitchen, pokey and cramped and unhygienic. Pictures pinned to the walls, hundreds of photos and postcards and cuttings. All of elephants. Every one.

And in the corner, sticking out from under a desk at a most unnatural angle, one long, twisted leg.

A long, twisted leg in a blue wool stocking and a dirty white sneaker.

Pernille's sneaker.

CHAPTER 25

A K!ller

Frederik wanted to throw up. The tramp had murdered Pernille and there was no way of escape. These seconds would be his last. A floorboard groaned and the tramp moved closer, breathing down his neck. It was his turn to perish.

The tramp held him by the collar.

Bent down awkwardly and peered beneath the desk.

"Girl!" he exploded. "What are you doing down there?"

The dead foot of the murder victim twitched.

The foot was still alive! Hope swelled in Frederik's chest like a hundred party balloons.

"Ah," came a muffled voice from underneath the desk. "Allow me to explain."

There followed a good deal of scraping and puffing before Pernille emerged, dusty, disheveled, but definitely alive. For now at least.

She smiled politely at the tramp. It wasn't convincing at all. "The thing is," she said, and then she registered Frederik at last and stopped in the middle of her sentence.

"What?" the tramp waited, furious.

"Melon!" said Pernille. "Fancy seeing you here." She gathered herself, somewhat sheepishly. She had no wounds, no missing limbs. She hesitated for a moment, helped herself to a seat, crossed her long legs one over the other, and attempted to appear prim.

"The boy's name is Melon?" said the tramp. "What kind of a name is that?"

"It isn't Melon," Frederik said.

"What's your name, then?"

"No. Yes. Melon. That's right." He dropped his eyes and stared in terror at the tramp's giant boots, smeared and stained.

Pernille cleared her throat. "Now, sir. I want you to

understand that Mr. Melon and I have friends in high places. Official friends. And relatives! They are no doubt looking for us as we speak. I advise you to let us go immediately."

"No. Tell me what you were doing underneath the desk," the tramp countered, bending down to take another look.

"I was looking," she said, "for ventilation. That's all. It's terribly stuffy in here."

The tramp raised himself to full height once more, and he had rather a lot of that. "You were trying to *escape*."

"Certainly not," said the girl. "Escape is the coward's way out. A true romantic heroine would… Well, she would… Well, I would have to think about that. On whose authority, may I ask, are you here in the first place anyway? No one's, I'll bet. Have you been sleeping up here? The place is a disgrace. And who are *you*, a trespasser, to detain two innocent, paying customers of the zoological gardens?"

Frederik brandished his annual card. "One of us paid," he said.

"The zoological gardens," the tramp growled, "are *shut*. Paying customers are supposed to have left. And there's nothing innocent about you two. You're up to something. What are you doing snooping around in my house?"

Frederik tried to swallow but now it didn't really work.

"Your house?" Pernille said eventually.

"Yes," the tramp erupted. "*My* house, you little vermin."

"I really rather doubt," said Pernille, her hands folded over her knee, "that this house is *yours.*"

Frederik risked a glance around the room. Unwashed clothes and crockery. Cuttings and magazine pages pinned to every inch of the walls. Pictures of elephants in the savannah, in the circus, in zoos, in parades. Hindu gods with elephant heads, as the shopkeeper had described. Woolly mammoths. Someone was living up here. Someone was using it as a hideout. Someone crazy, someone obsessed with elephants. A guru? No. A killer. Hiding from sight in the pyramid roof, a fugitive from justice.

The tramp slammed a fist on the desktop and sent a mug clattering onto the floor. "It *is* my house," he roared. "*My* house!"

Pernille ducked and yelped. Frederik skittered toward the wall, searching for gaps, anything. There was nowhere to go. Pernille was caught in the corner between an old sink full of unwashed plates and the inward slope of the ceiling.

"*My* house," the tramp hollered again, and the very

floor beneath Frederik's feet seemed to tremble. They had to escape! Run. Scram. Vanish. Vamoose.

And then Frederik's eye fell on the rifle.

It was leaning against a dresser, near the stairs. It was as long as Frederik was tall. It had a wooden stock and a telescopic sight.

And it all became sickeningly clear in an instant.

The tramp was going to shoot the mayor.

Her Ladyship would be gunned down in full view of the Royal Zoological Society's extraordinary general meeting.

He was hiding up here in the roof, waiting. For her.

They had to get out. Had to raise the alarm and stop the assassin.

"Hello! Come in! Come in!"

Everyone froze.

The voice was high and shrill. It came from somewhere down the stairs, from below, from the public hall of the elephant house.

For a very long moment, all three of them—Frederik, Pernille, and the homicidal tramp—stared at one another.

Nobody moved.

Nobody dared.

"Welcome, welcome. Take a seat."

Someone was down there! Several someones. Chatter and the scraping of chairs.

Quick as a cat, Pernille kicked out with one hard, pointed toe and caught the tramp on the shin. He howled and staggered, caught a fleshy thigh on the counter, howled again, and turned to rub at his rump.

Frederik threw himself forward, grabbed Pernille's arm, and tried to haul her clear. But the tramp was quicker than he looked. He gripped her shoulder and pulled her the other way, wrapped a hand around her face, and covered her mouth. Frederik ran at him punching and puffing. His little fists pounded deep into a fleshy midriff. The tramp grabbed the back of his neck, twisted him around, and suddenly everything went dark. He couldn't breathe. He tried to shout, but he was lost in the folds of an evil-smelling sleeve. He felt himself sinking toward the floor, overpowered, at the mercy of an enormous, grubby killer.

CHAPTER 26

The Taste of Blood

The tramp's face filled Frederik's entire field of vision. It was red and blotchy, with bloodshot eyes. The tramp laid a fat finger across cracked lips. "Shhhh. Be quiet." He leaned in even closer and muttered, through wonky, unbrushed teeth, "Or this could end very badly for you both. Do you understand?"

Frederik managed a nod. His voice wasn't working. Nothing was working—not his breathing, not his brain.

But he was, unexpectedly, alive. He had wrestled his head from under the tramp's stinking jacket. It had taken an age. He had no idea how much time had passed. But he

hadn't been suffocated. Not strangled or gutted or crushed. The tramp had set him down heavily, but he was unbroken. He had taken a deep breath the moment he was free, ready to holler his heart out. But the tramp was right there, right in front of him, glaring. He had hesitated. And once he hesitated, he lost all his courage. There was such a hubbub downstairs that no one would have heard him anyway. Muffled voices, lots of them. Sounded like hundreds. Chairs scraping on floor tiles. Chinking glasses, bursts of laughter, a whine of feedback from a microphone.

Frederik turned his head, very slowly, nothing sudden. Looking for Pernille.

She was pinned to the floor by the tramp's other hand. Her eyes were open. Very wide. She was looking at him. She was shaking.

He waited for the tramp to glance away, and as soon as he did, he gestured with his head toward the gun.

She nodded and widened her eyes even more. She had seen it too. She understood. The esteemed members and patrons of the Royal Zoological Society were gathering beneath them, entirely unaware of the deadly threat. They *had* to raise the alarm.

The tramp lifted his hand and Pernille skittered into the corner, pulled her knees to her chest, and wrapped her arms around her shins. She scowled at the tramp in fear and hatred.

The tramp seemed to fill the room. He was enormous. He wiped his dribbling nose on his sleeve, and it wasn't clear which one ended up dirtier.

Frederik edged underneath the table, hoping somehow to protect himself. He stretched his fingers toward Pernille's, but she was out of reach. She widened her eyes and blinked and widened them again. Like she was trying to signal something. But what?

The tramp thumped heavily across the attic to the dividing wall. Crouched. Hooked his fingers around a brass ring set into a floorboard. Pulled.

A single square panel, perhaps a foot along each edge, dislodged itself from the floor. The voices below were instantly sharper. The tramp knelt and put his face to the hole, staring down at the crowded hall beneath.

Frederik filled his lungs again, to shout for help, but what stopped him this time was a man's voice, from down below in the public hall.

"Ladies and gentlemen of the Royal Zoological Society!" The chatter died quickly away. "This evening's extraordinary general meeting is in session. I am deeply honored to introduce our guest and speaker, Her Ladyship Kamilla Kristensen, mayor of Frederik's Hill!"

Loud applause leaked up through the floorboards. The tramp flinched away from the spy hole with a scowl. He stared suspiciously at Pernille and then at Frederik. He drew a single filthy finger across his lips to signal silence. The rifle was no more than a yard from the tramp. This little hatch in the floor would give a clear shot at the mayor, and she wouldn't know a thing about it. She would fall dead in front of the whole zoological society. And if Frederik tried to stop it, what would happen? He'd be first! He'd be shot! He'd be dead in an attic in an abandoned building in the zoo and no one would ever find his body.

Something touched his foot and he jumped. Pernille's toe. Her leg was stretched out across the floor. She did the thing with the eyes again, and this time jerked her head toward the gun or the door or both—it was hard to tell. Her eyes were big and blue and scared. She moved her lips as though saying something.

What? he mouthed.

A giant finger pinned his shoulder to the kitchen cabinet—a giant finger on the end of a stinking sleeve.

"Stop conspiring!" the tramp growled in Frederik's face from point-blank range. There was a waft of evil dinner. Pernille withdrew her shoe in a hurry.

"Wasn't," Frederik croaked. It was all his dry mouth was capable of.

"Don't!"

From the open hatch the clapping gave way to a woman's voice. Low and clear.

"Thank you, yes, thank you. Patrons and benefactors of the zoological society, I am *so* pleased to join you tonight to continue our preparations for a vital local endeavor."

"Mama!" Pernille cried out. It echoed in the vaulted roof. M-mah. M-mah.

"Be *quiet!*" hissed the tramp, and he turned a murderous glare on them both.

"My International Midsummer Festival will bring the whole world to our door," said the voice of the mayor from downstairs.

"It's my mama!" And Pernille was getting to her feet,

completely ignoring the giant homicidal hobo filling the width and height of the attic.

"Where?" said the tramp.

"Wait!" said Frederik, terrified she was going to get herself shot or disemboweled or a messy combination of both.

"Frederik's Hill shall be elevated onto the global stage!" the mayor announced.

Applause drowned out the thud of Pernille's feet as she accelerated toward the hatch.

"Don't *interfere*!" the tramp howled, lunging after her.

She darted for the gap between the kidnapper and the wall.

"No!" the tramp hissed, grabbing her and spinning her around the edge of the room.

"Don't!" Frederik wailed.

And then something struck him.

Pernille was not doing what the tramp expected her to do. She was doing exactly the opposite. And the tramp was completely distracted. And if the tramp was distracted, he wouldn't be able to shoot the mayor!

He jumped to his feet to join in. Couldn't for the life of him think of anything unexpected enough.

There was more applause and noise from below.

"Help!" Pernille shouted, throwing herself toward the open hatch. "Mama!"

"Get away from there!" the tramp exploded, slamming his feet down directly in Pernille's way. He thumped the hatch back into place, sealing up the gap. The floor shook with the force of it.

And shook.

A low rumble in Frederik's ears, vibrations rippling across the room, and it occurred to Frederik that this could not be the tramp's fault. The floor and the cabinet and the table were *actually* shaking. The dirty plates in the sink were rattling. The rumble of the train! Again!

The tramp was looking wildly from side to side, disoriented, afraid.

And then Frederik knew. He knew exactly what to do!

"Earthquake!" he shouted. "Help! Help!" He staggered theatrically from side to side. "Help!" He grabbed at the tramp's beastly overalls, the very last thing the tramp was expecting. "Help! Help!" he shouted, right in the old man's face. "Earthquake! An *earthquake*!"

"No," the tramp panicked. "It's them! The *zombies*!" He

curled his enormous body into the wall and covered his head with his arms, making noises like an injured dog.

"Run!" Frederik threw himself at Pernille and pushed her toward the stairs. "Go!" His shoulder banged against the rifle. It fell with a shocking clatter and tipped over the top of the stairs. He reached but got nowhere close. The rifle was sliding on its side, down the stairs and around, down and around.

Pernille galloped after it.

Frederik followed her. He bashed the walls as he spiraled downward, caught his knee on the doorframe. Everything hurt. His chest, his knee. He stumbled.

Tripped.

Pitched headfirst into the open space of the whitewashed hall and landed with a terrific crash.

The rifle on the floor a few feet ahead of him.

Pernille in a heap.

He wheezed.

The taste of blood in his mouth.

He lifted his head.

And more than one hundred well-dressed grown-ups with glasses of wine and their mouths wide open stared back at him over their shoulders.

CHAPTER 27

You Know Who I Am

They looked over their shoulders and down their noses at Frederik. Every one of them. Middle-aged men in suits and ties. Elderly women in dresses and floral scarves. Not an empty seat in the hall, apart from either side of Henrik Hotdog, who was being carefully avoided. These people were not the hot dog type. They were the finger food, foie gras, guinea fowl type. They were the elite of the Hill. The well-to-do. Business owners, TV celebrities. Gretchen Grondal too, Frederik noted. Rows and rows of them, aloof and affronted. Staring. In silence. At him.

"Help!" he managed, but it didn't come out with

anywhere near enough force. He raised his head. Cleared his throat. Tried to overcome the concussion. He flung a finger toward the staircase. "Up there! He's up there!"

"*Whom?*"

Her amplified voice rang around the high walls of the elephant house. Frederik clambered to his knees and peered between shoulders, and there, at the head of the hall, looking down across the audience, he found her.

A confident posture—upright, powerful. Waves of white hair gathered behind her head. Dressed in elegant charcoal gray. Her chain of office heavy about her neck. Her Ladyship Kamilla Kristensen, the mayor of Frederik's Hill. A local legend. The borough's chief executive for longer than he had been alive.

"Tramp," Frederik sputtered. He grabbed the back of a chair, to the alarm of a matronly benefactor of the zoo. He hauled himself to his feet. "Your Ladyship! Please!"

As she stared at him, it was as though the sea of heads between them melted away, and only he and Her Ladyship remained. She swept a wayward strand of hair from her face. Her calm, clear voice rang over the room like a bell. "Who are you, little boy?"

Frederik. Frederik Sandwich. That was who he was. He opened his mouth, but no name came out. Time had slowed to a crawl. As though the room were in slow motion. "Get down!" It escaped his lips before he knew it was coming. "Get down! Or you'll be killed!"

One hundred simultaneous gasps, people twisting in their seats, the nearest instinctively flinching away. From Frederik. "No!" he shouted. "You must understand!" And now his voice was back, and it came out very loud indeed. "The gun! Look!" He pointed to the rifle on the floor.

Someone screamed. And right away, another. Chairs were screeching on the tiles as the back row tried to back away.

"He's got a gun!" A very thin woman was pointing at Frederik and shouting at the top of her lungs. "He's got a *gun*!"

"No, no!" said Frederik. "Let me explain!"

The orderly rows of chairs became a tangled confusion, obstructing one hundred people as they tried to go in contradictory directions. Men in suits and women in dresses were trying to climb over the chairs with glasses of wine in their hands, and it wasn't going well. There were cries of dismay, rude exclamations, clattering, spillage, and lots of falling over.

"Wait!" he called.

"He's going to kill us all!" the woman yelled.

Frederik reached for the rifle but thought better of it. What if it went off? The mayor was staring at him over the heads of the crowd. To her side, a small man, someone important from the zoological society, and a middle-aged lady in an ostentatious hat were trying to wedge themselves under the table. Only the mayor remained standing. Dignified. Defiant. High of brow and straight of back.

"It's not what you think, Your Ladyship," he shouted. "We are here for you."

Her composure cracked. She looked suddenly alarmed.

"No, no! Not to kill you. The killer's upstairs!"

Her Ladyship ducked.

And then all light and sound and feeling were abruptly muffled.

Frederik found himself bowling sideways, unable to see, with a mountain of cloth and flabby flesh squashing him flat to a very hard floor. He banged his head. Couldn't breathe. Couldn't holler for help. Overwhelmed by a horrid stench. The smell of old hot dogs. He wriggled and struggled and pulled his head back into the light, took a huge gulp of air.

Henrik Hotdog was sitting on him.

Sitting on him!

Holding the rifle!

"Help!" wailed Frederik. "Get him off me!"

One hundred fearful, fully grown adults stared back and did nothing at all.

"Get off my *friend*!" Pernille's voice cut through the confusion like the beam of a pocket penlight. All eyes darted her way, and Frederik was smothered all over again, greasy kitchen overalls in his face and a mountain of stomach pressing him flat. There was darkness. Stars. Pernille's sneaker wandered into focus and out again. He flapped his arms and Henrik Hotdog toppled off him in a pile, swearing and spitting. Pernille's enormous blue eyes loomed into view, extremely close.

"Lemon!" she said. "Please tell me you're alive!"

But before he could answer, two strong hands took him under the arms and hoisted him upright. "Borough Detectives Department," a low voice growled in his ear. "Don't move." His captor was a hundred feet tall and his eyes were as cold as the frozen sea. Another, in an identical business suit, loomed at his side.

"Mortensen! Martensen!" called the mayor. "Bring him where I can see him. At once."

He was marched to the steps at the front of the hall, the shaken members and benefactors parting and eyeing him with horror.

Her Ladyship rested her fingertips on the table and stared intently at Frederik. "*Who* are you?" she demanded to know.

He took the time to catch his breath, to collect himself. The danger had not yet passed and only he could make her see.

"Your Ladyship," he began, trying to keep the wobble out of his voice but sounding incredibly small in that vast, echoing space. "I am very sorry. Really! But there is a man. He is upstairs. At this moment. He means you harm. He has harmed you before."

The mayor's eyes darted involuntarily to the door through which they had so recently crashed. And was there a flash of recognition? Of understanding?

"A tramp," Frederik prompted. "A murderer!"

Her eyes narrowed. Her lips pursed. "What are you talking about, child? A tramp? I don't allow *tramps* in my meetings! Whatever next? And where did you get that gun?"

"I didn't touch it! It's his! It belongs to the killer! Don't you remember?"

"Remember what?"

"The train crash! The underground train crash on Frederik's Hill thirty years ago!"

It was as though the oxygen was sucked from the room entirely. No one breathed. No one dared. They were held spellbound by Her Ladyship's face, which was cycling through a range of lurid colors. Red. Then blue. Through crimson to purple. Her eyes were wide. She remembered! He knew it. He had got through to her at last. She gazed directly at him.

"Thirty years," she whispered.

"Yes."

But what was happening? Something was wrong. She tilted her head to the hatted lady under the table. "Explain," she growled.

The woman emerged, immediately awkward, flapping her hands for no clear reason, attempting to fan herself. "Well," she said. "Well, Your Ladyship. Perhaps we should talk"—she glanced toward the spellbound audience—"somewhere *private* about that?"

The mayor remembered where she was. She gave a slightly embarrassed smile to the zoological society. "Quite. Indeed." And she narrowed her eyes at the woman once again. "But I will *expect* an *explanation*."

"I can explain!" Frederik yelped. "I know all about it—the crash, the attempt on your life! He's back! I know what he has been doing. But please, Your Ladyship, you must stop him! Send your men!"

"How do *you* know about it?" She seemed very displeased. And mostly with him!

"The library! The newspapers!"

"*Newspapers?*" She glared afresh at the woman in the hat, who shrank beneath its brim. "I ordered them destroyed!"

"There are rules, Your Ladyship," the woman whispered back, so quietly that only the mayor and Frederik could hear. "We did what we could within the constraints of what is proper and allowed."

"No!" Frederik exclaimed. "Please! You don't understand. It was him! The tramp. *He* doctored the newspapers. He was trying to cover his tracks. So he could return undetected and get his revenge—on you, Your Ladyship. On the whole of Frederik's Hill. He caused the earthquake!"

Well, any oxygen remaining after Frederik's previous outburst disappeared in nanoseconds.

The mayor's face was thunderous. "There was no *earthquake*," she spat, and now there was something entirely different in her eyes. Something cold. Something dangerous.

"No," he said, remembering suddenly the need for discretion, to keep the earthquake quiet for the sake of her festival. "Of course. Not an earthquake, no. But *please*, Your Ladyship! He is up there! Who knows what he will do next?"

"Be quiet!" Her Ladyship pointed a finger at his head. "Be *quiet*!"

An unbearable dryness clamped his throat. He felt like his face was going to pop off with the pressure. Why wouldn't she understand?

"Ladies and gentlemen," she said, turning back to the microphone. "Please, please, accept my most profound apologies for this disturbance. Gather yourselves. Take a moment."

She gave the room time to settle. She weighed her words. "As I was saying before this interruption, my International Midsummer Festival will bring global attention to Frederik's Hill. The heads of state of several nations are invited. And VIPs from across the country." She paused for maximum effect. "And, I know you'll be thrilled to hear, Her Majesty Queen Margaret."

There was a collective gasp and absolute hush. The Queen! She had their complete attention now.

"But there are those," the mayor went on, "who would undermine our moment in the limelight. Nefarious factions. Malcontents." And she gave a pointed glance toward Frederik. "I have cause to believe that criminals are at large. In the dead of last night, I observed two figures emerging from a strictly *prohibited* area beneath Municipal Hall."

Another gasp, and mutters of outrage.

"Interlopers! Or actually outerlopers, to be exact. One of them was tall, the other short. Please memorize that description and be vigilant. One tall, one short! They must not be allowed to disrupt our international festival in any way! They must be identified and caught."

What felt like a grapefruit had embedded itself in Frederik's gullet. He tried to gulp but couldn't. One tall, one short. Frederik and Pernille. It was suddenly deeply important that no one made the association. That no one saw them together. He glanced back, couldn't help himself, wondering where she was hiding.

She wasn't.

She was marching boldly toward him, tangles of white hair bobbing around in her wake.

"Go away!" he hissed.

But she ignored him. Blanked him entirely. She marched to the steps and stood directly before the mayor.

Her Ladyship's eyes grew as wide as saucers as she stared down at Pernille.

"Listen to me!" Pernille demanded. More gasps from the gathering. She had dared to raise her voice to the mayor! "My small companion is telling the truth. If you won't listen to him, then listen to me." She paused. Raised her face in defiance, hands on hips. "You know who I am. I know you do."

CHAPTER 28

Bang

Her Ladyship the Mayor stared down at Pernille, speechless. She seemed unsure of what to say. Gripped by some colossal inner turmoil. She narrowed her eyes as though trying to remember something long forgotten. She tilted her head to one side as though considering a different theory entirely. Then she craned forward, over the table, examining Pernille in a kind of silent shock.

"You know who I am," Pernille repeated, and a hopeful smile at last spread over her lips.

Her Ladyship breathed in and kept on breathing in for

longer than ought to be possible. And then she let it all go in a single, sudden sigh.

"Such insolence," she said.

"I prefer to think of it as strength of character," Pernille replied. "And we both know who my strength of character comes from. Don't we?"

She waited.

And waited.

Her voice caught. Vulnerable suddenly. "Don't we?"

The mayor scowled and set her jaw. Folded her arms. Blinked. "No."

"No?"

"I don't have the first idea what you're talking about, young lady. But I know this: my orderly borough will not be disrupted by delinquents. I will not tolerate it. I will not stand for it! Who do you think you are?"

"You know who I am," Pernille pleaded.

Her Ladyship shook her head as though tossing something aside. "I do not. I have absolutely no idea. And I will not tolerate insolence, defiance, or anything else. Least of all from unwanted outsiders."

"Unwanted?" Pernille mumbled, deeply wounded.

The mayor lowered her voice so only they could hear. "*Look* at you, girl! Just *look* at you. A mess! Untidy. Slovenly. And that complexion. You're not one of us!"

Pernille jerked her face away as though she had been slapped.

Frederik stared, astounded and appalled. He reached out to Pernille, took her arm. She seemed to be collapsing in on herself.

"How dare you!" he shouted, turning back to the mayor. "What a terrible thing to say!"

But Her Ladyship wasn't listening.

She was staring at him.

And then at Pernille.

Then him again.

"One tall and one short!" she said. "It was you! You are the criminal outerlopers from last night!"

"We are loyal citizens," Frederik said. "Loyal to Frederik's Hill and to you, Your Ladyship. We came here to save you."

"I saw you escaping my tunnels." She dropped her voice to a whisper. "So *that's* how you know about the railway!"

He couldn't think. Couldn't make sense of what was happening. It was so unexpected.

Oh! Unexpected. Yes!

"Mortensen! Martensen!" ordered the mayor. "Take these criminals aside." And she pointed directly at the elephant cages lining the enormous hall. The two detectives, impossibly tall, reached out to take hold of them both.

"Pernille!" he hissed. "Do the *opposite* of what they expect!"

But Pernille just stood there, deflated and crushed. All her sparkle extinguished.

And it made him furious. More furious than he had ever been. He *had* to do something unexpected. He glanced wildly around and saw nothing. There had to be something.

BANG!

An enormous bang. Incredibly loud. From the back of the room. Something hummed past Frederik's ear at terrific speed. There was shrieking and panic. People stumbling, throwing themselves to the floor. The unexpected had happened entirely of its own accord. Well-to-do women and men were cowering, terrified, under their hands, as though their hands would somehow protect them from what was unmistakably the crack of an assassin's rifle.

In the chaos, he reached for Pernille. She was shaken but alive.

The mayor was uninjured too. "You see?" he wailed at her. "I told you!"

And then his eye was drawn to the mayor's lady assistant. Her ostentatious hat was in her hands. A thick, sticky liquid was dribbling down her forehead. She was holding the hat away from her in shock. There was something stuck in it. Some kind of dart. An enormous dart, like a doctor's syringe, with a flamboyant, fluffy, pink tail. What *was* that? A tranquilizer dart? Was the tramp planning to *tranquilize* the mayor? Why would he do that? To kidnap her?

The sprawling, wailing people parted. At the back of the hall, even more avoided than ever, stood Henrik Hotdog. He was staring in frank surprise at the rifle in his hands. A little wisp of smoke curled out of the end of it.

"Erm, ah," he said. "My bad, Your Worthyship. I was trying to help. Trying to turn it off. Thought it might nudge that catering contract my way, if you know what I mean."

Gretchen Grondal lurched into view and threw a hand in the air. "I must object! Your Ladyship! That contract should be mine."

And then, without warning, another explosion! The door to the stairs burst open again and smacked into the wall. The glass shattered. People scattered. A massive shape appeared in the doorway.

The tramp.

He thundered into the room and sucked in a rasping lungful of air. "Where's my gun?" he roared, his eyeballs bulging out of his head. "Who fired my gun?"

His eyes fell upon Henrik Hotdog.

Henrik Hotdog didn't seem the type to be easily intimidated. But today was a day for the unexpected. He offered the rifle rather meekly in the tramp's direction.

"No! *No!*" Frederik yelled. "Don't give him the gun! No! No!"

One of the tall detectives went running at Henrik, shouting warnings. So did the tramp. Henrik tried to duck out of the way, but he wasn't nimble, and the three of them collided. Hands were grabbing. Punches exchanged. The gun was ripped out of Henrik's hands and Frederik couldn't see who had it now. There was shouting and bumping. Heads cracked against stone. And now Frederik was running too. Not thinking, just running and yelling. He tipped himself headlong into the melee, kicking and grasping and gasping for air. "Get the gun away from him! He wants to kill the mayor! Or kidnap her! Or something!"

But the tramp had the gun, and Frederik couldn't get close. The tramp had the rifle entirely in his control. He tore himself out of the tussle, knocking Henrik and Frederik aside and brandishing the weapon in the air. "Listen to me!" he hollered. "All of you! Listen to me!"

"Duck!" Frederik hollered. "He's going to shoot!"

The two detectives hit the tramp at the same instant, one from either side, driving their shoulders into his midriff, collapsing him, winding him. He went down like a landslide, demolishing another row of chairs and toppling several onlookers.

"Stop it!" The mayor's voice rang out over the room like a siren. "Stop it *now*! I command you to *stop*!"

There was thrashing and grunting, some misplaced punches, a number of words not normally used in polite society gatherings.

Frederik scrambled to his feet. The others too, disheveled and flushed, one of the detectives gripping the gun, the other the tramp.

"Silence!" the mayor demanded.

Frederik lurched forward. "It's him!" he shouted, pointing at the tramp. "He's a killer! He's the culprit!"

"I know who he is!" the mayor boomed, her face red with rage.

"He's been down in your secret tunnels! You remember him, don't you? From the train crash. He's the one who caused the train crash."

"*I* didn't cause the train crash!" the tramp yelled out. "*She* did!" And he pointed a dirty finger directly at the mayor.

"Now he's back!" Frederik was shouting. "He came to kill you!"

The mayor seemed to grow another foot taller. She towered above them all. Her face furrowed with fury. "*Enough!* All of you! You have said *enough*! Entirely *enough*!"

A weighty silence descended. Frederik's vision had gone all blurry. There was a ringing in his ears. Traumatized members of the zoological society hugged the walls. "Take them aside," the mayor growled. "Take all of them aside and I will fix this once and for all."

They were marched behind bars—Pernille, Frederik, and the tramp. Into one of the giant elephant cells at the edge of the hall where the benefactors wouldn't hear them. The floor was rough stone. The walls were whitewashed brick and rusting metal. Nothing was in the cell except for a tatty bench.

The tramp was cursing. He glared at Frederik. "I told you to keep quiet. Now you're done for. We all are!"

The mayor swept into the cell like a storm, her hair awry, her chain of office askew across her bosom.

"So," she said, turning an icy glare at the tramp. She looked so slight before him, as though he could blow her away with a single smelly belch. But it was he who took a step back. "These children are with *you*? These outerlopers? Suddenly it all makes sense. You're trying to sabotage me. *Again.*"

"It wasn't us!" Frederik yelped.

The mayor beckoned to her hatted assistant. The poor woman shuffled into the cell, head bowed, and peeped at the mayor from underneath her brim. The tranquilizer dart was still embedded in the hat, a tuft of vibrant pink and a mostly empty syringe. It must have squirted all over her hair. Glistening serum was smeared down her cheek.

"Table a motion," the mayor commanded her. "A motion to remove the chief elephant keeper of the Royal

Zoological Gardens from his post." She looked directly at the tramp. "For gross negligence. For rank incompetence. For deliberate sabotage of municipal affairs! Effective immediately. Put it to the vote. Now. This evening. While we have the quorum. And the witnesses."

Spit bubbled between the tramp's lips. "No! You cannot fire me. You can't! You have no *right*. I never sabotaged you. You sabotaged me! You had me arrested!"

The mayor encroached on the tramp again, forcing him back toward the wall. "I allowed you to keep your position," she said. "For thirty years. I showed commendable mercy considering the damage you caused. We made an agreement. An agreement you seem to have forgotten!"

"Agreement?" he spat back. "Blackmail, you mean. Keep quiet or else. Keep quiet or lose my job and my home and everything. The elephants. My lovely elephants. You held them over my head like a sentence. For *years*. What kind of a woman are you?"

Elephants? Frederik stared bewildered at the tramp. Then at the mayor. Then the tramp again. Pernille too had been shaken out of her heartbreak. Her head twitched from side to side, trying to grasp what was going on.

The tramp was an elephant keeper?

The *chief* elephant keeper? The chief elephant keeper of the Royal Zoological Gardens of Frederik's Hill?

The *tramp*?

"But he had a gun," Frederik said. And then felt immediately foolish. Of course he had a gun. A tranquilizer gun. Who else would have a tranquilizer gun? Who else would live in an elephant house? Who else would cover their wall with elephant pictures? Who else would have clothing smeared with dung?

"Oh!" he managed. "*Oh!*"

CHAPTER 29

Upside Down and Inside Out and Back to Front and All at Once

You're the elephant keeper!" Frederik said, staring wide eyed at the tramp. "The *chief* elephant keeper."

"Shut up!" the mayor ordered. "Stupid child." Then she rounded on the tramp again—or elephant keeper, as it now turned out. She gestured at the chaos beyond the bars. "You know how long it took to get those idiots out there on my side? *You* caused this chaos. Now *you* will take the blame."

"No," he snarled. "No, I won't. This is all your doing, Kamilla. Always has been."

"You will call me 'Your Ladyship'!"

"I'll call you whatever I want. You don't scare me." But he seemed to flinch anyway, to back away once more. "I'll tell them everything. I'll tell them the truth. They'll never elect you again. You can wave bye-bye to your fancy office, your big black car, your ridiculous chain. And all those perks. All the privileges. Your pompous lackeys and your pampered life."

"You wouldn't dare!" She spat like a cat, back arched, teeth bared, hands curling into claws. "You'd be finished forever!"

"And so would you!"

They glowered at each other as though there was no one else in the room. This mountainous man and this trim woman, each as dangerous as the other, but in such different ways. And now it was clear that Frederik and Pernille had got it wrong. All of it. Every detail. This wasn't what they had thought. This was the opposite of all they'd expected. It was like being turned upside down and inside out and back to front and all at once.

"So who caused the earthquake?" Frederik asked, bewildered.

"Zombies," the elephant keeper hissed. "*Her* zombies."

"But it was the train, surely? It nearly derailed. The underground train."

The mayor tipped her head back and laughed out loud. "The train? Is that what you came up with? A *train*? You little buffoon."

"It was."

"It was not." And the tone of her voice, her absolute certainty, hit him like a slap.

"You know," he said. "You *know* what caused it."

"Of course I know! I know everything that goes on, on Frederik's Hill. I control it. I arrange it."

"You arranged the earthquake?"

"No, you idiotic boy." She stepped even closer, lowered her voice to a hiss. "I arranged a test of the fountains. That's all. In preparation."

"The fabled fountains?" Pernille murmured. "Of Frederik the Tenth?"

"A grand surprise for my midsummer festival. They were to be restored. Renamed in my honor. To honor me! Do you see? It was water. Not an earthquake. Water!"

"Such a pity," the hatted assistant said. "Who was to know the pipes were so corroded? That they'd vibrate like that?"

"Shut up!" the mayor snapped.

The woman ducked and her ostentatious hat slid off her slippery hair. She set it on the bench for safekeeping.

The elephant keeper plucked the tranquilizer dart from the hat and inspected it closely. "Don't listen to a word," he said. "She lies. She always lies. To save her reputation. To bury the truth. It was zombies. Down in the pipes. I heard them moaning." His voice cracked. He wasn't joking. "I was down there with them."

"What?" the mayor exploded. "You? You were in the pipes?"

"I heard them coming for me. Their terrible moans, their howling as they came for me and my elephants."

"*Elephants?* You took elephants down there?"

"I was taking them for a walk!" he snapped back. "Because of you!"

"*Me?*"

"Because of your inhumane rules. Your ridiculous festival. Your big self-serving ego trip. You stopped the animals from exercising outdoors. *Your* orders!"

"They stink. I will not have them stinking near the Queen!"

"That's months away!" He loomed over her, even redder in the face than usual. "Elephants need exercise. In the wild they walk all day. Hundreds of miles, nonstop. You can't lock them up like that."

"So you took them into the pipes?" Frederik said, still very confused. "How?"

"Through the big hatch," said the elephant keeper, as though Frederik was dim. "Near the penguins. And then what happened? Ask her! She knows." He pointed directly at the mayor. His voice dropped to a whisper. "They awoke. Her miserable monsters, her drear nightmares, hidden in the darkness for decades. I heard them. Coming for my elephants. The pipes were shaking, juddering like they'd break apart."

"It was water, you idiot," barked the mayor.

"Zombies!"

"Water!"

"Zombies!"

"And you ran," Frederik realized. "You ran."

"Of course I ran!"

"And so did the elephants."

"They stampeded! They were terrified. Trapped

underground in the dark, pursued by zombies! What would *you* do? They charged like they'd never charged before. I was almost trampled. They were swaying and bashing against the sides. Couldn't see where they were going. And all the time, the sound of those evil creatures getting closer, breathing down our necks."

"Did it sound like this?" Frederik asked. He cupped his hands across his mouth and mimicked the mournful noises he and Pernille had heard in the pipes just hours before.

"Yes! You heard them too?"

"We heard something."

"And then we were crashing through the Cisterns," the keeper said, shuddering. "Through all that damp and rust and decay. That's where they live! That's where the zombies dwell!"

Pernille stepped to Frederik's side, spoke softly into his ear. "So *she* is saying that water was flooding through the pipes."

"Yes. And it made them vibrate. Made them moan and howl."

"Exactly like the noises we heard."

"And then the elephants stampeded. Through the pipes under Frederik's Hill. Frightened. Disoriented. Bashing against the sides of the pipes. And we were woken up by an earthquake that couldn't possibly have been." He lifted his face to the elephant keeper, quite forgetting now to be afraid. "It was your fault," he said. "The earthquake." He pivoted to face the mayor. "And it was yours."

The mayor's face folded into an evil scowl. "You will keep quiet about this, you weasel. I will make sure of that! What are your names?" She looked at Frederik, then Pernille. Little flecks of spit sat along her dainty lower lip.

"I do not know," Pernille replied. There was something new to her voice. An edge. "I do not know what my true name is. But I have learned one thing. My name is not Kristensen. My name is not yours. That is terribly clear. I am no child of yours."

The mayor stared at Pernille, a little vein pulsing at her temple. "What are you blathering about, girl? Are you a half-wit?"

"No!" snapped Frederik. "No, she is not!"

"And what is *your* name?" inquired the mayor, turning toward him with nothing but malice.

"Enchilada," he said without any hesitation, without any respect, and, at last, without any fear.

"Oh, is it?" the mayor scoffed. "I rather doubt that. Let's see. Who is here tonight who might know you?"

"No one," he told her, brave now. Answering back. No longer willing to be bullied. "No one at all."

But the mayor was turning her back on them, barging past the detectives, leaning though the bars to address the members and benefactors. "Can anyone identify this delinquent boy?" she called out.

And from the crowd, instantly, stepped the one person, the one interfering busybody who could.

Gretchen Grondal.

"Oh no," Frederik whispered.

CHAPTER 30

Padma

The café proprietor bustled into the shabby cell in her Sunday best. She elbowed the elephant keeper aside and stood before the mayor. "*I* can identify him, Your Ladyship."

"Tell me."

Frederik's body had gone cold. Pernille's face had turned a shade of green.

Gretchen Grondal straightened herself, pursed her lips, took a deep breath. Paused. "Actually, just before we go there, Your Ladyship, might we clarify your choice of caterer for the grand event?"

The mayor gaped back at her.

"After all the bother this evening," Miss Grondal went on, "I'd hate to see the decision delayed. We must be at our best for the Queen, don't you think?"

The elephant keeper towered behind Miss Grondal, glaring down at her. *Everyone* was glaring at Miss Grondal.

"Yes, yes," said the mayor. "Fine. The contract is yours." She poked the hatted lady. "Write that down. Café Grondal will cater the midsummer festival. Now. Who is the boy?"

Miss Grondal smiled in triumph. She cleared her throat. She threw Frederik a vicious sideways glance. "I don't know his name," she said.

Frederik's stomach flip-flopped. Was there hope?

"But I know exactly where he lives."

"Where?" the mayor demanded, agitated, her chain of office swinging side to side.

"He lives," said Miss Grondal, "just along the street from..." And then she gave a peculiar yelp. Clutched a bony hand to her behind.

The elephant keeper edged away.

Miss Grondal's lips parted. She tried to say something.

It might have been "flurgle." Her voice faded, her eyes glazed. She dropped to her knees on the stone floor, and then pitched face-first into the ostentatious hat, crushing it flat, her rear end sticking up in the air.

And there, protruding from her derriere, was a large dart, with a flamboyant, pink, fluffy tail.

"Whoops," said the elephant keeper. "How did that happen?"

"You've tranquilized my caterer!" shrieked the mayor. "What have you done?"

The elephant keeper shrugged. "She'll be fine. There was hardly any left. She'll wake up in, ooh, about twenty-four hours, I should think."

"That's the final straw," Her Ladyship spat. She turned to the detectives. "I want all of them behind bars!" But just as she said it, the bars gave an ominous rattle. A shudder ran through the floor. And then another. Frederik knew what that must be. The train coming around again. And he knew what to do.

"Earthquake!" he yelled. And quick as a whippet, he was past the mayor and the two detectives, and out into the hall. "Another earthquake!" And sure enough, the room was vibrating rather impressively. Dust and cobwebs drifted from the ceiling. The bars were humming. The locks were rattling. Chairs were skittering on the tiles.

"Oh, mercy me!" a woman exclaimed.

"An earthquake!" Another.

"Save us!" hollered a third.

"Run!" Frederik yelled. "Get out of here! Before the pyramid roof collapses!"

And here came the elephant keeper, shambling through the bars and staggering listlessly about. "Zombies!" he was shouting. "They're coming again! Rising from the belly of the earth!" The man was clearly nuts, but that was just fine. Let him rant. Let him stumble around and collide with people and chairs and everything else. Let the zoological society descend into mayhem once more. It wasn't expected. It was just the opposite. And this was their chance. He turned to find Pernille at his shoulder, a grim expression on her face but upright and all in one piece.

"Come on!" He took her hand.

"Hey! You!" The detectives were wading after them through the crush.

"Run," said Frederik. "No! Not to the exit. That's what they expect. The other way!" He steered her toward the wrong end of the hall. "Duck low!" They struggled forward, against the tide. Up the steps and through the bars, throwing the gate wide open. The detectives were faltering, swept backward by the flood of people heading the other direction.

A roar behind them. The tramp, still ranting. "No! Don't go down there!"

But Frederik kept going. Just paces now from the big rusty door that led to the tunnel that led to the railway below. And the nearer he got, the stronger the vibrations. The more the floor shook.

And then, in an instant, the shaking stopped.

Completely.

And Frederik stopped. Pernille at his side. Both of them astounded.

Because the big rusty door that led to the tunnel that led to the railway was sliding sideways. Inching open. Shoved aside by a stout, gray trunk. And peering down through the gap from the tunnel beyond was one round, black eye. Long, thick eyelashes. A wall of deep-set wrinkles.

The sliding door kept moving, clanged against its frame, opening as wide as it could go.

And Frederik Sandwich found himself face-to-face, or

rather face-to-nose, with an elephant. A very large, very real, very right in front of him Indian elephant.

The elephant squeezed itself through the archway and took three deliberate steps inside the hall. As its feet hit the floor, the floor vibrated—in a way that was now very familiar.

"Oh," Frederik murmured. "Oh, I see."

The elephant kept coming. It filled the whole space in front of them, blocking their way to the tunnel, forcing them back toward the crowd, the detectives, the mayor. Trapping them. It looked from side to side as though gently amused by the chaos, all those people in their finery, falling over one another. It made a curious little huffing noise and picked at Frederik's toes with the funny, flappy fingers at the end of its trunk.

"Padma!" The elephant keeper, breathless, pushed past them. He threw his hands flat onto the elephant's flank in a kind of hug. "*There* you are! I've been worried sick. I've been searching for you for two days. I looked *everywhere*! The railway, the pipes, even the library. Anywhere I could get to underground. I thought the zombies had you. I've been going crazy!"

The elephant looped its trunk around the keeper and caressed his straggly hair.

"What the devil is *that*?" the mayor was shrieking from somewhere behind them. "*Another* elephant?"

"You left one down there," Frederik finally understood.

"We got separated," the keeper said. "In the stampede. In the dark." He rested his cheek against the elephant's. "There, there. Calm now. You're safe."

The elephant made a contented gurgling noise at the back of its throat.

"There's been an elephant loose underground," said Pernille. "Ever since the earthquake."

"It wasn't an earthquake," the keeper said.

"No, it wasn't," said Frederik. "And that shaking today wasn't the train." He stared, amazed and a little afraid, at the giant creature towering over them all. "It was Padma."

The elephant looked back at him for a moment. Then slowly, lazily, she swung her trunk and started walking, brushing them aside, heading for the hall. With every footfall, the floor trembled. The members of the zoological society panicked and wailed and scattered all over again.

The mayor stepped forward, furious, her hesitant detectives at her flanks. She tried to bypass Padma, but Padma turned a full, agile circle, tipped her head back, gave a deafening trumpet, and let loose a flood of pee that washed and frothed across Her Ladyship's shoes. Her Ladyship screamed.

Frederik took Pernille's elbow. "Quick. While they're distracted."

He pulled her through the doorway and into the tunnel, gripping her hand. They ran, dipping downward, ever steeper, bending away from the elephant house into the belly of the hill. The tunnel closed over them, barely enough light to see their way, the floor rough and hazardous. Twisting around and back, corkscrewing deeper, deeper— and suddenly an opening, an archway. A wooden platform with a layer of old straw. A mound of poop—Padma's.

And a train.

Deep underground, an old blue train with a disgusting diesel engine and tatty curtains at its windows hissing hoarsely to itself.

They sprinted for the carriage. But then Frederik remembered that the doors opened automatically. And all these doors were closed. A sudden lurch of panic and a sudden jolt of the train. The diesel vented filthy exhaust and prepared to leave the station.

"No! Wait!"

He tugged at handles. Pernille bounded down the boardwalk, leaping at every door she passed. None would open. The train was moving, steel scraping on steel, carriages bumping one another. Frederik lost his footing and fell in the straw and dung. There remained no part of him that wasn't bruised. The train gathered pace, belching fumes. Pernille persisted. Checking doors, checking again, ever closer to the back of the train, rattling handles until she reached the last. She put her foot up on the step. Carriages were rolling fast past Frederik's face. Pernille was swept along the platform toward him. The door she was holding tumbled open and out. She somehow clung on, swung around, angled her long, long legs inside. She flung out a hand and yelled, "Jump, lemon. Jump!"

And he ran. For all he was worth. The end of the platform and a redbrick wall racing closer and closer. He grabbed at her fingers, one last burst, got a toe to the footplate. She hauled him up with just seconds to spare. The train thundered into darkness. Frederik on the carriage floor, panting, bruised, exhausted.

And free.

CHAPTER 31

Welcome to the Club

He gradually put himself back together as they rattled through underground night.

Rubbing sore elbows and dusting off straw, they ventured along the train. It would take only minutes to Frederik's Hill. Things that seemed so strange only yesterday, the chintzy lamps and threadbare furnishings, were now enormously reassuring. They sat by a window and caught their breath, watching darkness clatter by. In no time at all, the train hissed to a halt in the disused porcelain factory, one stop from safety. A fine, white dust filmed every surface

of the station. The decorative urns. The white-and-blue tiles and their floral motifs.

Frederik watched Pernille's reflection in the glass. "Are you all right?" he asked.

"She is not my mama," she whispered. "She is not."

"No," he said.

Her eyes met his. "Then who is?"

"Tickets please!"

They almost jumped out of their seats.

"Oh! You again?" The train conductor bowled along the carriage, checking her watch, frowning severely from under the peak of her cap.

Frederik put his head in his hands. "No!" he moaned. They had escaped. Almost made it home. Now they were caught. By the borough!

And then, unexpectedly, the conductor sat down beside them with a great sigh of neglected cushions and a little puff of dust.

"How nice," she said. "Let's chat. It gets rather lonely down here on my own. Young Mr. Enchilada, wasn't it?"

"No, it's Sa… No. Yes. Enchilada."

"And Miss *Kristensen*, as I recall? Like the mayor."

"No," Pernille said with passion. "That is not my name and it never was. I was very mistaken it seems. Very mistaken."

The train conductor smiled. "Oh, I *am* relieved to hear it. You seem such a delightful young lady. I couldn't believe you might be connected to anyone so hateful."

"She *is* hateful," Frederik exclaimed. "Full of hate and spite. She said terrible things to Pernille. Awful things. Hurtful things."

"Pernille?" said the conductor. "That's your real name, is it, dear? How pretty. I'm no fan of Her *Lady*ship, as I mentioned to you before. Our paths don't cross anymore, I make sure of that. But her shadow hangs over me all the same."

"She is not the woman we were led to believe," Pernille said.

"She caused the earthquake!" Frederik said. "We thought it was your train."

The conductor chuckled. "This train loops the Hill unnoticed every thirty-four minutes, my dear. If we caused earthquakes, I imagine we'd be very much noticed."

"You told us you almost derailed in the night. Shook like a roller coaster, you said."

"Oh, that. Yes. The line was suddenly flooded, you see.

And there was an elephant! We almost hit it. Can't imagine what it was doing on the track." She gave a small, sad sigh. "Don't suppose I'll ever know."

"Of course!" said Frederik, another piece tumbling into place. "You *were* part of the earthquake. The water, the elephants, *and* the train, shaking like a roller coaster. All at the same time!"

The conductor stared at him doubtfully. "What are you talking about, dear?"

"There's a vast cover-up," he said. "And the mayor is at the heart of it. Every piece of it comes back to her. Not the tramp. Not you. The water was her fault, the elephants in the pipes, the stampede, the shaking train—all her. It's as though everything we have ever been taught about Frederik's Hill is a *lie*."

"It probably is, dear. The mayor is head of education. I tremble to imagine what the schools of this borough teach young children. Her own version of events, of that I'm sure. Her own agenda."

Pernille was shaking her head slowly side to side. "She was my role model all my life. *All* my life."

The conductor watched her carefully. Sympathetically.

"Oh, she is very convincing, my dear. Very polished. She bamboozles us all."

"I was bamboozled," Pernille said. "That's it exactly. What a fool."

"No. You mustn't blame yourself."

"My father works for her," Frederik realized, appalled.

"So do I, dear. On Frederik's Hill, everyone does in one way or another. She has her talons in everything. But thankfully, somehow, she forgot to shut down my railway. Too consumed with her own public image, no doubt."

"She forgot? You're saying she *meant* to shut you down but didn't remember?"

"Yes. Or I'd be out of a job. Ole the engineer too, poor soul. Her Ladyship, you see, long ago, threw a spiteful tantrum and ordered the stations locked and the public barred. After a while, the whole borough simply forgot we existed. But no one thought to take us off the timetables."

Suddenly, it dawned on Frederik: "And rules are rules," he said.

"Precisely. So long as we're on the timetable, we've got to keep the train running, haven't we? We've been looping the borough for decades without a single passenger. Until you.

And I must say it's rather lovely to see someone. Ticket or no ticket." She rested her head against the tatty seat and sighed.

"Tell us about the lighthouse," Frederik said. "Did people just forget that too? Because the train didn't stop there anymore?"

The conductor's face darkened. "That was Mayor Kristensen's doing. That was deliberate. And vicious. Old Mayor Bergholt was her predecessor. Such a kindly man. He loved that lighthouse. Looked after it well. It was built to show off the fountains, you know, but they had failed, clogged up with scale. So Mayor Bergholt lit up the park with it instead. Then Miss Kristensen came along. She wanted power. She wanted him gone. She claimed that the lighthouse was a danger to aircraft. Mayor Bergholt took the blame, they shut the lighthouse down, and guess who was elected in his place."

"She's evil," Pernille said.

"She slapped that clock on the side of the lighthouse and then, quietly, she turned it to her own purpose."

"As a clock tower?"

"As a watchtower. It's her personal lookout post. So she can watch. All the time."

"Watch who?" Pernille asked.

"Everyone. Me. You."

Pernille gave a bitter little laugh. "And all those years I hoped she might be watching over me."

The train made impatient hissing noises but didn't move—not yet.

"She's having a massive row with the elephant keeper," Frederik confided. "Right now. At the zoological society."

"The elephant keeper?" the conductor said, sitting up with a start.

"We thought he was a tramp."

"Tramp?" A dreamy haze glazed the conductor's eyes, a faraway look as though she were falling asleep. "You mean Rasmus?" She seized Pernille's hands between her own. "Tell me, dear. Was he well? Was he hearty? Hale? Whole?"

"Who? The tramp?"

The conductor laughed. "A tramp indeed. A *tramp*. He's far from that, my dear."

"He's filthy," Pernille argued. "Filthy and smelly. And he harangued us. He was unspeakably rude. Bad tempered and objectionable."

"Yes," the conductor said fondly. "That's the fellow.

Of course, he wasn't always so grumpy. He was calm, kind. Many years ago. Before his nightmare at the hands of the mayor." A thundercloud seemed to pass before her face.

"You mean the disaster?" Frederik asked. "On the railway? Of course. You'd know all about that!"

"As if I could ever forget."

"That's why she closed the line, isn't it? There was a crash. An elephant was involved. She had the keeper arrested."

"And I never saw him again," said the conductor in gentle despair. "I so wanted him to be mine."

She got to her feet, distracted, disconsolate. She wandered away to the door. She pulled down the window and blew on her whistle suddenly and loudly. The train jolted, started to slowly roll, folding into the darkness of the tunnel.

"My dear Rasmus. My long-lost love. She accused him of attempted murder. A vicious lie. It didn't stick, thankfully. But he became paranoid after that. Disturbed. Afraid to come down here, beneath the ground. It scares him silly."

On cue, the lamps went out again. For a few seconds the train rattled and shook in absolute darkness. Then one by one, back came the lights.

"And my whole life is down here," she said. "I work down here. I sleep down here."

"In that little office at Municipal Hall station," Pernille realized. "We saw your footprints."

"So I never see him," she concluded, forlorn.

"He was down belowground two nights ago," said Frederik. "In the pipes. With his elephants."

"Was he? *Was* he! Well, that explains the one we nearly hit."

"They were part of the earthquake. They stampeded. Because of the noises. The elephant keeper thought it was zombies. But I'm sure it's the pipes. There's something wrong with them. They make a horrible sound. I don't think they've been looked after."

"Just like my railway," said the conductor. "That's Her Ladyship again. Anything out of sight is left to decay. All the underpinnings of Frederik's Hill—the pipes, the foundations, everything is crumbling. All the money goes to her pet projects. That overpriced elephant house she built while the wonderful old one falls apart. And this absurd international festival. Such hypocrisy. She *hates* foreigners. Detests them. But she'll do anything to look good. Anything to get reelected."

"Then she's risking our safety!" Frederik said. "That's so irresponsible. There's an old chimney outside my house. I'm frightened it's going to fall on us."

"She has created an illusion," the conductor replied. "An illusion of perfect order. And the whole of Frederik's Hill believes it. They *want* to believe it. They follow her every rule."

"Rules are for fools," Pernille said.

"In this borough, I'm afraid they often are."

"We should tell people," Frederik said. "We should expose what she's doing."

"No one will believe ill of the mayor. She's everyone's darling. And anyone who crosses her pays a heavy price."

"Then we're powerless," Pernille said, dejected again. "We really are nothing but unwanted outsiders."

"Welcome to the club!" She tilted her head back and her hat fell off. She laughed. "You're not alone, my dears. There are more outsiders on Frederik's Hill than you might think. Me, for one. Rasmus too."

Pernille looked up at her. "And the shopkeeper, Mr. Ramasubramanian."

"We should band together," Frederik said. "Work as a team."

"Perhaps," the conductor chuckled. "Yes, perhaps. Well, you know where to find me now."

"Except we're not allowed down here," he said. "Not without a ticket. Rules are rules."

"Indeed they are. And I know your name." She leaned toward him and gave a conspiratorial wink. "Don't I, Mr. Enchilada?"

With no warning at all, the train swung sharply to the right, out of the ground and onto the main commuter line. Streetlights. Cars. Then down into shadow again. A crowded platform, faces, people. It howled to a stop and the doors flew open with an unholy clatter to receive no one.

The conductor stood up on tiptoes and bellowed at the very top of her voice, "Frederik's Hill! Frederik's Hill! This train terminates here!" She bustled them off their seat. "Off you get. Run along. The Frederik's Hill Municipal Branch Line understands you have a choice of service carriers, and we thank you for riding with us today. Please remember to take all personal belongings with you. Thank you. Goodbye."

She ushered them down the steps to the platform.

Travelers eyed them with suspicion as they tumbled from an empty train, clothing covered in dirt and dung and dust. The doors banged shut like a chain reaction, one after another. The conductor leaned from the window and blew a shrill blast on her whistle.

As the train stuttered out of the station, she shouted back, "And if you see my Rasmus again, give him my love!"

CHAPTER 32

Two Half Orphans

Yellow buses followed yellow buses. Traffic lights changed from red to green and back. People in scarves bicycled by and ignored them entirely. There were no pointing fingers, no police. No sniffer dogs sniffed, no helicopters hunted. Just old, dry leaves in the wind and evening on Frederik's Hill.

"Nothing is different out here," Frederik said, a little bewildered. He saw it as though for the very first time in his eleven or thereabouts years. "Nothing has changed. The conductor is right. Nothing will alter. Nothing will be said. Everything will be exactly the same. Except us."

"And we are completely changed," Pernille whispered, breathless with the weight of it. "My mama is *someone else*. Perhaps I am an orphan."

"No. No, you're not. You have the upholsterer. You're only half an orphan." Somehow it didn't come out as helpful as he had hoped.

They walked quickly up the street, ready to duck into any doorway at the first sign of detectives. They checked over their shoulders time and again.

Venkatamahesh Ramasubramanian pursued them from his doorstep. "Did you follow your guru? Did he lead you to enlightenment?"

"Kind of," Frederik told him. "An answer anyway."

"And was it an elephant?"

They stopped. Turned back. "Yes! Yes, it was!"

The shopkeeper's eyes widened with surprise. "Really? My mother was correct?"

"A female Indian elephant," Frederik told him. "Called Padma."

His mouth fell open. "That was my mother's name."

Pernille walked back to him. "Did you say that both your parents passed away?" she asked him gently.

"Yes. Sadly that is true."

She looked at Frederik. "The only one who got it right…"

"Was an orphan," he finished.

Pernille wrapped the little shopkeeper in a sudden hug. "Thank you for helping us," she told him. "And welcome to our club!"

He backed away, flustered and flushed.

They cut along alleyways to the square by Frederik's house. Made sure it was deserted. They watched his front door. Was it safe? They were a party to secrets now. Secrets and lies. They couldn't tell a soul. No one would believe them, outsiders, immigrants. They would have to keep a low profile.

"Down here," he told her. "Let's stay out of sight."

The path wove through the bushes into the overgrown center of the square. The great brick chimney reached to the clouds. He listened at the door of the old brick hut. No voices. The nasty neighbors were all at home in front of TV and warm food. Frederik realized he was terribly hungry.

The old lantern was inside the doorway. He tried it. A feeble glow among dark shadows. Pernille peered down the steps that led underground into blackness. "What's down there?"

"A cellar. And a pipe."

"A pipe? Another one? Where does it go?"

"Through my parents' closet."

Pernille eyes grew wide in the lamplight. "Isn't that dangerous?"

"Has to be if no one is maintaining it. This chimney too. It could topple onto my house."

"Let's look." She took a stair down. Her ankles and calves were lost in a puddle of darkness. "Bring the lantern." The murk reached her knees, then her midriff. A narrow beam pierced the black like a spear. Her pocket penlight. "Another entrance to the underworld." She shivered. "No zombies, I hope."

He started after her. The lamp swung and shadows lurched. He almost lost his balance on the stairs. The fat, rusting pipe bulged from the wall. She tapped it with the pocket penlight and it rang dull like a broken bell.

"A doorway!" she said.

He had forgotten about that. It was sealed by bricks, but it was a doorway all the same. Must have once led under the porcelain factory.

She dug the end of the pocket penlight into the

mortar and tried to prize the bricks from the wall, to chip her way through.

"What are you doing?" he said.

"Yes," said a voice at his shoulder. "What are you doing?"

Frederik yelped, couldn't help himself.

Erica Engel sneered from halfway up the stairs. Another pair of legs beside her.

"If it isn't Fiddle-lick the spy," said Frederik Dahl Dalby.

"And the weird girl," Erica added.

"They've stolen our lantern. Go get the gang."

But the gang was already arriving. Voices upstairs. Erik the Awkward, Calamity Claus. More feet on the stairs. They were trapped underground, no way out.

"We've caught some thieves," Erica told the newcomers. "Cell phone anyone? Call the police."

"No!" Frederik's mouth had operated without his help.

"Something to hide?" Dahl Dalby sneered. "Guilty secrets?"

"You idiots!" Pernille marched to the foot of the stairs and used her height to full advantage. Erica and Dahl Dalby stepped back, startled. Pernille grabbed the lamp from Frederik and waved it in their faces. "There are secrets *everywhere*! All around! An epidemic of lies!"

"Give us our lamp," Dahl Dalby snarled at Pernille. "You don't belong here, you *foreigner*."

"Don't you *ever* talk to my friend like that!" Frederik roared, and let's remember Frederik was a really rather short individual, previously unprone to outbursts of any kind. He launched himself at Frederik Dahl Dalby, his fists clenched and his jaw set hard.

He was stopped by the flat of Dahl Dalby's outstretched hand to his forehead. "One more step, Sandwich, and I bang you into the ground like a peg."

But Frederik wasn't about to back down. He pushed his head hard against Dahl Dalby's fist. At the edge of his vision, he saw something arcing through the air extremely fast. Pernille's pocket penlight hit the lantern with a smash and a tinkle of tiny pieces of glass. There was sudden absolute stillness and dark.

Seconds oozed by like lava.

"They broke our lamp," said Erica's voice from somewhere nearby. There was a scuffling noise and a beep. The glow of a cell phone held in the air. Silhouettes. Fists raised.

"Aaaagh!" Frederik yelled as loud as he possibly could,

his throat rasping. "There's something down here!" He rapped his knuckles against the pipe. It rang eerily.

There were nervous gasps from the stairs.

"They're in the pipes!" he yelled. "Help us! Aaaagh!"

Pernille began to moan and wail. "*Zombies!* The earthquake awoke them. They're here for our *souls!*"

"They're here for our souls!" Erica repeated, panicking, and the light was suddenly heading away up the stairs.

"Wait for us!" Erik the Awkward and Calamity Claus said, scrambling, trying not to fall.

Frederik threw himself after the silhouettes and trailed the tips of his fingers down the back of Dahl Dalby's leg.

Dahl Dalby squealed and bolted for his life. Footsteps smacked on the steps, out of the hut and away, through the bushes, twigs snapping, frightened whimpers.

They waited a long time. Alone underground, in darkness.

Alone but brave.

Alone and thrilled with themselves.

"Thank you," said Pernille. "Thank you, Frederik."

"Nobody speaks to my friend like that."

"Nor mine."

"You remembered my name," he realized. "You've never remembered my name before."

"It somehow won't stick," she said. "It seems too common a name for such an uncommon individual."

"Thanks," he said. "I think."

They climbed the steps warily. The neighbors were long gone. A blue evening folded around the enormous chimney. They picked through the bushes, emerging across from his house.

"My father's bicycle," he said.

"I don't see a bicycle."

"Exactly. He must still be at work. At Municipal Hall. He was called in this morning to help the search. For the two intruders. Us."

She rested her elbow on his shoulder. "Then it seems we are both half orphans."

"I'm sure he's not *dead*."

"But gone all the same. Stolen away by the mayor."

He felt suddenly ill at ease. In the distance, the Municipal Hall clock chimed the hour.

"Actually," she said, "I'm rather delighted."

"What? Why?"

"Because two half orphans makes a whole one. And that means you and I are fully equipped to solve any mystery."

They crept to the corner and checked the street. No one was lurking, no shadowy figures. Nobody watching his house or hers. Just a few diners minding their own business in the window of Café Grondal.

"What should we do about the mayor?" he wondered. "She's putting everyone at risk, and for what? Her own glory."

"We'll think of something. There are others we can call on. We're not alone." She contemplated the dark street in silence. "And I won't be stopped," she said. "I will find my mama."

"Then I'll help."

She grabbed his elbow, squeezed it hard. "Would you?"

He was grinning. He tried his best not to. He didn't want to look like an idiot. "You need your other half."

She draped a long arm around him, and this time he didn't think to shrug her off. "That's wonderful news," she said. "You're rather good company, you know." And she sauntered away, up the street, entirely conspicuously, toward the ramshackle workshop with the sat-upon roof.

"See you tomorrow, then?" he called after her.

"Count on it, currant," she replied.

Acknowledgments

This book couldn't possibly be if not for Suzanne Brahm, Phoebe Kitanidis, Peter Kahle, Lyn Macfarlane, Kate Madrid, Brian Bek, Jayant Swamy, our dear Billee Longuski Escott, and my helpers from Turquesa class at Montessori Children's House, Redmond.

Thank you also to Annie Berger and Jim McCarthy for shaking Frederik awake.

To all our friends in Denmark: the happiest, grumpiest, most decent land there is.

And to my mum and dad, Karen, Steve, Milo, and—most of all—Sam, for believing in my nonsense every day. I love you all.

Read on for a sneak peek of Frederik and Pernille's next adventure in

FREDERiK SANDWiCH and the MAYOR Who Lost Her MARBLES

Two Short Weeks Before Her Ladyship the Mayor's International Midsummer Festival

O n Frederik's Hill, by King Frederik's Park, in an orderly office high in Municipal Hall, there stood a woman. A serious woman who people took seriously. A woman of position, a woman of influence. A woman in a very bad mood.

"What the flipping festering devil," she demanded, "is *this*?"

She flung the morning newspaper across her desk. Her desk was enormous. Enormous and orderly. The paper

slid all the way across and fell off the other side, onto her enormous, orderly floor.

Two tall detectives in identical, dark suits stared down at it. One of them cleared his throat a bit, but neither dared say a word.

Her Ladyship the Mayor of Frederik's Hill turned to her window in a fury. Her window was broad and high and spotlessly clean. Frederik's Square lay below her, a fountain at its heart. The finest stores and delicatessens lined Frederik's Avenue. Factory chimneys and the massive cylindrical vats of the brewery stood proud on her skyline. All Her Ladyship's sources of revenue, taxes, and tariffs stretched before her. Frederik's Hill was an economic marvel, respected near and far. Thanks to her. It had taken years. Decades, in fact. Patience and grit. A ruthless attention to detail. And no one—*no one*—was going to get in her way. Not now, when she was so tantalizingly close to her long-awaited payoff.

One of the detectives retrieved the paper. "'Children Flee from Zombies,'" he read.

She placed her fingertips on the enormous, orderly desk. "Zombies!" she shouted.

"I didn't know we had any," the detective said.

"We don't!"

"No. Right. Of course. But it's on the front page, Your Ladyship."

"I am well aware which page it's on," she barked. "If I say there are no zombies, there are no zombies. I want to know who allowed this to be printed."

The detectives shuffled their feet and inspected their toes.

"Thomas is the editor, ma'am, as you know. Thomas Dahl Dalby. But he's loyal. Totally trustworthy. If Thomas says there are zombies, there must be something behind it. I wonder where he got the story from?"

Her Ladyship scowled and snarled. "From a fantasist. A saboteur. I want the presses stopped. I want the internet erased. Is that clear? I want all references to zombies rooted out and removed!"

"Like before, ma'am? With the earthquake?"

"Yes, exactly like that. This is catastrophic."

Her Ladyship caught herself grinding her teeth again. Her dentist had told her not to. But despite her position, and all her staff, it seemed she *still* had to take care of everything herself.

Two months had passed since an accidental

"earthquake" almost derailed her glide toward international fame. Every day since, she had fought to restore the right impression. Impressions were everything. She'd appeared on TV, online, and on the radio, radiating calm. She had spoken at meetings and malls, paving the way for her Midsummer Festival, creating a buzz. Souvenir programs were in the stores. Little, decorative flags fluttered above the streets. All mention, all *notion*, of anything untoward had been thoroughly buried. Her mishap with the fountains, her humiliation in front of the zoological society—silenced. Until this!

She drummed her fingers on the polished desktop.

"That moronic elephant keeper," she growled. "He was mumbling about zombies. Remember? During that nightmarish meeting at the zoo."

"We don't talk about that, Your Ladyship."

"I know we don't! But now we do. Is that clear?"

"Erm, right. Yes. No."

"Did it leak?"

"No, Your Ladyship. No, no. Not a peep."

"Are you sure?" Far too many respectable voters had witnessed her embarrassment—nasty kids confronting her, an elephant peeing all over her shoes and her spotless public image.

"Absolutely. Definitely. We spoke to everybody who was there, face-to-face, one-on-one, eye-to-eye. Told them *exactly* what would happen if they talked. We put a lid on the whole thing. Sealed it up, ma'am. Sank it like an elephant in a lake."

She glared at the detective. Mortensen. Or was it Martensen? It didn't matter. "You got to *everyone* who was there? Without exception? What about that Hotdog hoodlum?"

"We caught up with him next day, Your Ladyship," the other detective said. "He parks his cart by the ice rink. He wasn't hard to find."

Her Ladyship stiffened. "He parks a hot dog cart by the ice rink? At the entrance to the Garden Park? The main entrance?"

"That's right, ma'am."

"That's entirely *wrong*!" Heat was rushing to her face now. Her jaw ached from the grinding. "My festival guests are going to use that entrance. The ambassadors, the foreign VIPs, the queen! I will not have a filthy peddler waving hot dogs at the queen!"

"Of course. We'll deal with that."

"Do it now!"

"We'll close him down, ma'am. Revoke his license. He'll never sell a sausage in a public place again. We should have thought of that before."

"You should have thought of that before!"

"We should have."

"You should have!"

She snatched the paper from the detective's hand and stared at the headline again.

"Zombies!" she yelled. "Again! And children!" And a thought struck her. A horrible thought. "There were children at the zoo. The ones who appeared from nowhere. The tall one and the short one. What about them? What happened to them?"

"Ah," said Martensen—or was it Mortensen? "Never actually identified, Your Ladyship. Actually. Tricky, that one, actually. Erm. Not seen since, you see. Long gone. Over the hills and far away. But they won't be back. They weren't even local. You could tell just by looking at them."

Her Ladyship glared at each detective in turn. "Then how did this *zombie* hysteria get out? Tell me that!"

"We'll find out, Your Ladyship. We'll track it to the source and deal with it."

"*Thoroughly*, this time."

"Understood."

"Ruthlessly!"

"Got it."

"You are authorized to use whatever means are necessary. *Whatever* means."

The detectives nodded, exchanged a glance, and were reluctant to meet her eye.

"Is there a problem?" she demanded. "Are you too squeamish for this? Mortensen? Martensen?"

"No problem, Your Ladyship. No problem at all."

"Then get on with it."

She turned her back on them, dismissing them with a wave of her hand. She watched from her window as buses and bicycles puttered by, far below, on her busy, prosperous streets. The morning haze was burning away. Flags curled in the cool summer breeze. Beyond the buildings, the long, green sweep of the Garden Park stretched all the way up to the castle on the hill.

Two more weeks.

Just two more weeks of preparations, planning, and publicity. Two short weeks until her International Midsummer Festival—the fireworks, the VIPs, fine local cuisine. No fountains, to her great frustration. She'd been forced to abandon that plan. But Her Majesty the Queen would be there, and the eyes of the world would fall upon Frederik's Hill—and on Her Ladyship, at last.

"Zombies," she muttered in cold fury. "Zombies!"

Nothing would get in her way. Nothing and no one.

CHAPTER 1

Reckless Miss Adventure

Muffin!"

Again?

"Yoo-hoo, muffin, dear!"

Seriously? It wasn't that Frederik Sandwich disliked Pernille's company. Wasn't that at all. But there was such a surprising amount of her company to cope with. He was heading home now. He'd said goodbye. He was hurrying down the pedestrian walkway from Frederik's Shopping Mall toward Frederik's Hospital. It wasn't the quickest route home, but it was out of sight of Municipal Hall. These days, they steered clear of Municipal Hall. Anyone might be watching from those windows.

"Let's climb the new observation tower," called Pernille.

"It's three hundred years old. It isn't new."

"But it's newly opened to the public."

"No. I need to go and do something."

"What thing?"

"Anything. A thing. Some things. Does it matter what things?"

"Everything you do matters to me, muffin. I've got your back. I am the marvelous Miss Adventure, and you are my sidekick. You may be a mini-sized, funny-talking misfit, but you are the Toto to my Dorothy, the sandwich to my soup."

"Good grief."

"Go on. It'll only take a few minutes."

The tower was dead ahead, a stout cylinder of brick-work, ancient lettering on its face. Narrow, arched windows were sparsely spaced around its sides. The mayor had opened it one week ago, part of her campaign to impress the world. A prelude to her International Midsummer Festival on Frederik's Hill.

"No. We can't," he said. "It's too risky."

The mayor was as popular as ever, the earthquake all

but forgotten. Hardly anyone understood how dangerous she was. She might have cameras up in that tower. Listening devices. Spies and informers.

"But it's so deliciously tempting," Pernille said. "Think of the views from up there, above the rooftops, looking out across the Garden Park."

And she was right. They'd be able to see the city beyond with all its spires and domes. Maybe catch a glimpse of the suspension bridge in the far distance, stretching over sea to another country.

"Just a peek, muffin. You know you want to."

"No. We can't. And my name is not 'muffin'. How many times have I told you?"

"But I like muffins. Much more than sandwiches. And I like you too. Ergo, de facto. Sorry, but there it is."

He hurried on, head down, hoping she would give up. He was done for today. Enough of her endless chatter. Apartment blocks rose six floors ahead of him. Early summer sunlight bounced off their windows. Raucous children ran around with ice creams. Bicycles whizzed by, freewheeling riders laughing out loud. Frederik kept walking. Didn't look back. Refused to.

Where was she now?

He wouldn't look. It would only encourage her. Was she behind him? She was bound to be. Right on his heels.

Bother it. Why wouldn't she give him a break?

He wheeled around. "Stop it!" he said. To no one at all. Just a wide-open space of concrete and lawn, children and cyclists, a tower. Where was she? What was she doing? Where had she gone?

Oh. There. Way over there.

A willowy figure, impossibly tall, her hair as white as winter snow and her skin a deep brown. You couldn't miss her, even from here.

She was ignoring him, hands behind her back, staring up from the base of the tower to the very top.

She made her way to the public entrance, rummaging in the folds of that baggy thing she was wearing. For what? Coins? She never carried them. She wouldn't get in. They wouldn't let her. Not without paying. It wasn't allowed. Not even Pernille could spirit herself through a turnstile in daylight with all these people about.

He watched her dip her head and talk to the hazy face behind the glass of the ticket booth. Nodding, laughing, throwing her arms around happily. Dazzling them. She was dazzling them. Whoever was behind that glass was getting dazzled. He'd fallen for it himself a hundred times, and he still didn't know how. He resisted every time, but to no avail.

And then she was through, beyond the gate, waving goodbye to her brand new friend and disappearing into the base of the tower.

Frederik groaned out loud, put a hand to his head, and screwed his eyes shut. Anyone might be up there. People they needed to stay away from. Why was she always so reckless? They weren't safe yet. She *knew* that.

Just two months earlier, they had greatly disrupted a prominent public event. You never ever did that on Frederik's Hill. Ever. They had gone to the zoo with good intentions, to save the life of the mayor. But the mayor was not the role model everyone imagined. She had caused and then ruthlessly covered up an earthquake, and only Frederik and Pernille knew the truth. The mayor's detectives had almost caught them that night. An elephant had intervened, and a secret, underground train had swept them to safety. But were they out of the woods? No.

They'd lain low ever since. For more than two

months. Kept a low profile, stayed out of sight—and getting Pernille to stay out of sight was about as easy as hiding a lighthouse in a busy public street, a deception worthy of the mayor herself. The girl was like a beacon. You could see her from one hundred yards and hear her from three hundred, whether you wanted to or not. For Frederik, it was easy to pass unnoticed. He was short for his age and wholly unremarkable to look at. But Pernille Yasemin Jensen was as un-unremarkable as it got. She absolutely shouldn't go up that tower!

The top of it opened out to a viewing platform. People up there, of course. It was quite the attraction, especially on a sunny Saturday afternoon. He couldn't see her. Not yet. No mess of white hair among the others looking down at him.

Hold on.

Why were those others looking down at him?

The sun was bright, and he had to squint to figure out who it was.

Oh no!

And Pernille heading up there on her own!

He shielded the sun with the flat of a hand. Was he

right? Yes. Erica Engel. Hateful. Frederik Dahl Dalby, worse. And Calamity Claus, calamitous.

And when Pernille reached the top of that tower, it would be more than calamity. It would be bad words and bitter battle and all in public. Not low profile at all!

So now he was jogging. Not going home. Not getting the downtime he had hoped for. That wasn't happening. Instead, he was running over the lawn to the base of the tower and thrusting some money at the face behind the glass. How much? *That* much? To climb a tower? Were they serious?

Into the cool of a gray-walled passage. A tiled floor spiraling upward. Splashes of light from the narrow windows as he puffed uphill. Glimpses through glass of the mall in the distance. Trees. The back of the library. The upper windows of apartment blocks. The orange slope of the roofs. Chimneys. Sky.

"Wait for me," he muttered. "Pernille, wait for me."

He was out of breath. His face was hot. His footsteps slapped on the tiles. A door to the open air. He stumbled outside. He stopped, panting, no idea which way he was pointing.

"Flipper-rack." Erica Engel, his nastiest of neighbors,

emerged from the blaze of sunlight, sneering. "You're here too? They *are* letting their standards slip."

Frederik Dahl Dalby slimed across the viewing platform, looking down his nose. "Your weird friend is over there. We were just advising her to go somewhere else. Dangerous places, towers. Accidents happen. Don't they, Calamity?"

Calamity Claus was the most accident-prone individual on Frederik's Hill. He was leaning over the railings, paying no attention to the dizzying vertical drop. He gave a knowing chuckle and nodded.

At the far side of the platform was Pernille, arms folded tight, one leg crossed in front of the other, eyes narrowed in anger.

What had they said to her? He could guess. *Weird. Freak. Foreigner.* Or worse.

Are you all right? he mouthed.

She shrugged. Looked away. Wouldn't give the bullies the satisfaction of knowing she wasn't.

Air and sky all around them. A jumble of rooftops and chimneys. The uppermost windows of Municipal Hall, a couple of streets away. At its corner, a tall lighthouse that nobody knew was a lighthouse, a balcony halfway up its side, a clock above that, reading a quarter past three. And at the very top, massive screens of glass facing out from a green copper lantern house. Another of the mayor's dark secrets. It made him shiver. Who did she spy on from up there? Or more to the point, who *didn't* she spy on?

"Nothing to say, Flabby-wreck?" Frederik Dahl Dalby said, breathing down his neck.

"*Don't* mock my accent."

"What do you expect?" Erica laughed. "You can't even say your own name properly."

It was true. Frederik was almost twelve, and he'd lived here all his life, but he couldn't shake the traces of his parents' foreign accent. The local language was impossible. Nothing was pronounced the way it looked. *Pernille* rhymed with *vanilla*, *Claus* rhymed with *mouse*, and *Frederik* rhymed with nothing whatsoever. Was this his fault? No, it wasn't.

"I'll say my name however I like."

"Oooh! Look who's gotten all brave."

"Shut up."

"What are you going to do about it, Fiddle-rock?" Dahl Dalby said. "There are none of your imaginary *zombies* to protect you up here."

Frederik looked right into Dahl Dalby's eyes. "What did you say to Pernille?"

"Nothing she doesn't deserve."

"What does she deserve?" Frederik was getting angry. "Insults? And why? Because she's a tiny bit different from you?" He wasn't going to stand by and let them do this anymore. He'd scared them away once. He and Pernille. Trapped in the dark by a whole group of them. *Zombies*, he had shouted. *They're here for your souls*. And Frederik Dahl Dalby, Erica Engel, Calamity Claus, and the rest had fallen for it and fled like frightened lambs.

The memory made him smile.

"What?" said Dahl Dalby, instantly annoyed. "*What?*"

Erica Engel crowded in from the left. Pernille drifted their way. She'd seen he was outnumbered.

"Something to say to us, Feather-neck?" said Erica.

"No," Frederik sighed. He pushed between the bullies and headed for the railing. Calamity Claus watched him come, leaned back, and folded his arms in a way that was probably meant to seem threatening, lost his balance, and tipped over the railing, eyes wide, flailing for a handhold.

Frederik grabbed his hand and yanked him back to

the viewing platform. Calamity Claus fell hard on the stone, banged his knee, and yelped.

"You're welcome," Frederik said. He placed his hands on top of the railing and gazed into the distance, across the leafy trees of the Garden Park, up toward the summit of Frederik's Hill. Above the eighteenth-century castle, flags flapped in the breeze. The yellow stone was patterned with white-framed windows, sunlight splintering off the glass. Steep grass ramparts fell away from its toes to the boating lake below.

Beyond the castle, out of sight, hidden below a lawn so flat and featureless that no one ever asked, there was one more secret. An old secret. Older than the mayor. A rusting complex of water tanks, long forgotten. It fed a maze of pipes that wormed and twisted under the whole of the borough. Those pipes did not react well to water pressure anymore. And living very nearby was an addled elephant keeper, who firmly believed there was something bad inside those pipes.

Zombies.

The bullying neighbors didn't scare Frederik anymore, but they were cruel and unkind. They'd hurt Pernille, and they deserved whatever he could think up.

"You're right about the zombies," he said. Softly.

"What?" said Dahl Dalby, close behind him.

"What?" asked Erica Engel.

"There are no zombies here," Frederik said.

"No kidding," Erica scoffed.

"They don't exist," said Dahl Dalby.

Frederik ignored them. Continued to stare at the castle on the hill. "The zombies are up there."

Dahl Dalby, Erica, and Calamity Claus must have managed a full twenty seconds before they looked. He could tell how hard they were trying not to, gathered at the railing, faces frozen, blinking too much.

Claus gave in. "Up where?"

"Up there." Frederik nodded toward the castle and the hill. "In their subterranean lair."

"What lair?"

"There is no lair."

"He's lying."

"He's a liar!"

"No, he isn't." Pernille had joined them so quietly they hadn't seen her arrive.

It made Erica jump, and that made her mad. She glared at Pernille. Bared her teeth. "Weirdo," she hissed.

"When the zombies come," said Frederik, "they will come from up there. They will sweep down the hillside, striking whoever crosses their path, crushing all before them."

"You're making it up."

"If only I were."

Dahl Dalby laughed. He tried to make it dismissive, disdainful. But it wasn't convincing. He stared with Erica and Claus across the gaping space of sunshine and rooftops, treetops and hillside. Each of them suddenly paled.

"Anyway," said Frederik. "See you around." He took Pernille's arm, and the two of them slipped through the door to the top of the ramp.

"Dimwits," said Pernille.

"Halfwits," said Frederik.

"And you duped them again, muffin. Thank you for that. Let's visit someone more friendly. Let's get ourselves some half-price chocolate."

"All right, Miss Adventure," he chuckled. "Let's do that."

About the Author

Kevin John Scott is from England and has lived in some peculiar places. This book is about one of them. Today he lives near Seattle with his hilarious wife and son, some trees, and an occasional bobcat.